THERESA

By Barbara Cartland
and published by New English Library:

LOVE IN THE MOON
ENCHANTED
COUNT THE STARS
LOVE RULES
KNEEL FOR MERCY
FROM HATE TO LOVE
LIGHTS, LAUGHTER AND A LADY
BRIDE TO A BRIGAND
THERESA AND A TIGER
THE PERIL AND THE PRINCE
THE DEVILISH DECEPTION

THERESA AND A TIGER

Barbara Cartland

NEW ENGLISH LIBRARY

First published in Great Britain in 1984 by New English Library

First NEL Paperback Edition November 1985

NEL Books are published by
New English Library,
Mill Road, Dunton Green,
Sevenoaks, Kent.
Editorial office: 47 Bedford Square, London WC1B 3DP

Printed and bound in Great Britain by
Cox & Wyman Ltd, Reading

British Library C.I.P.

Cartland, Barbara
Theresa and a tiger.
I. Title
823'.912[F] PR6005.A765

ISBN 0-450-05815-8

THERESA AND A TIGER

WHEN THE Countess of Denholme dies, her daughter Theresa finds she owns a fortune.

She has lived a very quiet life in the country with her mother after her father, the Earl, left them for the gaieties and beautiful women of the Second Empire in Paris.

She is wondering what she will do alone, when her Uncle and Guardian, the new Earl of Denholme, tells her that as she is so rich, she is to marry his son. Horrified, hating all men because of her father's behaviour to her mother, Theresa runs away to France.

She obtains a job as a Chef in the isolated Château of the *Marquis* de Sare, which is situated in the Basses Pyrenees.

How Theresa finds the *Marquis* has a private menagerie, how after two years he comes home unexpectedly, and how Theresa changes him and his mind, is told in this delightful 353rd book by Barbara Cartland.

ABOUT THE AUTHOR

Barbara Cartland, the world's most famous romantic novelist, who is also an historian, playwright, lecturer, political speaker and television personality, has now written over 390 books and sold over 370 million books over the world.

She has also had many historical works published and has written four autobiographies as well as the biographies of her mother and that of her brother, Ronald Cartland, who was the first Member of Parliament to be killed in the last war. This book has a preface by Sir Winston Churchill and has just been republished with an introduction by Sir Arthur Bryant.

'Love at the Helm' a novel written with the help and inspiration of the late Earl Mountbatten of Burma, Uncle of His Royal Highness Prince Philip, is being sold for the Mountbatten Memorial Trust.

Miss Cartland in 1978 sang an Album of Love Songs with the Royal Philharmonic Orchestra.

In 1976 by writing twenty-one books, she broke the world record and has continued for the following seven years with 24, 20, 23, 24, 24, 25 and 22. In the Guinness Book of Records she is listed as the world's top-selling author.

In private life Barbara Cartland, who is a Dame of Grace of the Order of St. John of Jerusalem, Chairman of the St. John Council in Hertfordshire and Deputy President of the St. John Ambulance Brigade, has fought for better conditions and salaries for Midwives and Nurses.

She has championed the cause for old people, had the law altered regarding gypsies and founded the first Romany Gypsy camp in the world.

Barbara Cartland is deeply interested in Vitamin therapy, and is President of the National Association for Health.

Her designs "Decorating with Love" are being sold all

over the U.S.A. and the National Home Fashions League made her, in 1981, ''Woman of Achievement''.

Barbara Cartland's Romances (Book of Cartoons), her cookery book "The Romance of Food," and "Getting Older, Growing Younger" have been published in Great Britain, and the U.S.A.

OTHER BOOKS BY BARBARA CARTLAND

Romantic Novels:
over 370, the most recently published being:

Diona and a Dalmatian
Fire in the Blood
The Scots Never Forget
The Rebel Princess
A Witch's Spell
Secrets
The Storms of Love
Moonlight on the Sphinx
White Lilac
Revenge of the Heart
Bride to a Brigand
Love Comes West
The Island of Love
Theresa and a Tiger
Love is Heaven
Miracle for a Madonna
A Very Unusual Wife
The Peril and the Prince
Alone and Afraid
Temptation of a Teacher

The Dream and the Glory
(in aid of the St. John Ambulance Brigade)

Autobiographical and Biographical:

The Isthmus Years 1919-1939

The Years of Opportunity 1939-1945
I Search for Rainbows 1945-1976
We Danced All Night 1919-1929
Ronald Cartland (with a Foreword by Sir Winston Churchill)
Polly My Wonderful Mother
I Seek the Miraculous

Historical:

Bewitching Women
The Outrageous Queen (The story of Queen Christina of Sweden)
The Scandalous Life of King Carol
The Private Life of Elizabeth, Empress of Austria
Josephine, Empress of France
Diane de Poitiers
Metternich – the Passionate Diplomat
The Private Life of Charles II

Sociology:

You in the Home
The Fascinating Forties
Marriage for Moderns
Be Vivid, Be Vital
Love, Life and Sex
Vitamins for Vitality
Husbands and Wives
Men are Wonderful
Etiquette
The Many Facets of Love
Sex and the Teenager
The Book of Charm
Living Together
The Youth Secret
The Magic of Honey
Book of Beauty & Health

Keep Young and Beautiful by Barbara Cartland and Elinor Glynn.

Cookery:

Barbara Cartland's Health Food Cookery Book
Food for Love
Magic of Honey Cookbook
Recipes for Lovers
The Romance of Food

Editor of:

The Common Problems of Ronald Cartland (with a preface by the Rt. Hon. the Earl of Selborne, P.C.)

Barbara Cartland's Library of Love

Barbara Cartland's Library of Ancient Wisdom

''Written with Love'' Passionate love letters selected by Barbara Cartland

Drama:

Blood Money
French Dressing

Philosophy!

Touch the Stars

Radio Operetta!

The Rose and the Violet (Music by Mark Lubbock), performed in 1942

Radio Plays:

The Caged Bird: An episode in the life of Elizabeth Empress of Austria, performed in 1957.

General:

Barbara Cartland's Book of Useless Information, with a Foreword by The Earl Mountbatten of Burma.
(in aid of the United Colleges)
Love and Lovers (Picture Book)
The Light of Love (Prayer Book)
Barbara Cartland's Scrapbook (in aid of the Royal Photographic Museum)
Romantic Royal Marriages
Barbara Cartland's Book of Celebrities
Getting Older, Growing Younger

Verse:

Lines on Life and Love

Music:

An Album of Love Songs sung with the Royal Philharmonic Orchestra.

Film:

The Flame is Love

Cartoons:

Barbara Cartland Romances (Book of Cartoons) has recently been published in the U.S.A. and Great Britain and in other parts of the world.

AUTHOR'S NOTE

The evolution of the public Zoo really began in France under Louis XIV who approved £5,400 a year for the upkeep of his Menagerie at Versailles.

In 29 BC Octavius Augustus owned a collection of animals including 420 tigers, but it was Noah who assembled the first Menagerie, and the Ark, to put it mildly, must have been extremely overcrowded.

The ancient Egyptians, the Chinese, the Indians and the Romans all kept wild animals in captivity. In England William the Conqueror took over an already existing animal park at Woodstock near Oxford.

Julius Caesar had mentioned in the *Commentaries* that rich English landlords had parks in which they kept 'pets'. There is a record of a nobleman receiving a bear from William Rufus.

When the Prince of Wales (Edward VII) toured India in 1875-6 he returned with a magnificent collection of wild animals given to him by the Indian Princes.

The *H.M.S. Serapis* sailed from Bombay and the collection included two fully grown tigers, 'Motee' and 'Jahaun'. The sailors renamed them 'Moody' and 'Sankey'.

They were very ferocious but a young tiger and tigress 'Tom' and 'Nimmie' allowed themselves to be led through the streets of Bombay to the docks and boarded the ship as a sailor put it "just like Christians". Once aboard they were exercised every morning on deck. A fifth tiger cub was so fierce he was named 'Vixen'.

White tigers are very rare and a pair bred in India cost the Bristol Zoo in England, £8,000 in 1963. They are very beautiful and have ice-blue eyes.

Chapter One

1869

THE FLOWERS on the grave were already beginning to fade.

Theresa picked one or two of the dead carnations from the wreaths and told herself that tomorrow or the next day she would take them away.

Her mother had always hated dead flowers and she herself felt as if something beautiful had died every time she looked at one.

She put the little bunch of primroses which she had picked earlier in the morning on the head of the grave and remembered how her mother had always said every Spring:

"The snowdrops are beginning to show and so are the primroses! The winter is nearly over, and is it not lovely to think that the sun will soon be warm and we shall be able to spend a lot of time out of doors?"

The lilt in her voice had made Theresa feel that it was more exciting to be out of doors than inside, and she knew now that what she would miss more than anything else were the walks with her mother in the woods.

She would miss too the rides they took together over the fields, and she remembered the times when she was small when they would picnic by the stream and afterwards she would swim in the cool, clear water.

It was not only the things she could remember that were so painful, but the knowledge that she was now alone!

The one person she had loved, the one person who had understood what she was trying to say, who always gave her new ideas and what she thought of as new inspirations, was dead.

"Oh, Mama, how could you have left me?" she asked. "How am I to do without you?"

It was hard to hold back the tears that came to her eyes, but her mother had always said that it was wrong to be anything but dignified and controlled in public.

"In your position, my darling," she said, "you have to set an example to other people. Always remember that if you cheapen yourself and behave badly or commonly other people will follow you."

Theresa looking down at the grave, thought there were very few people who would look on her as somebody of importance and follow her example.

Ever since her father had left them and gone to live abroad she and her mother had stayed very quietly in the old Dower House to which generations of Dowagers had retired once their sons had inherited Denholme Park, which was always known in the village as the 'Big House'.

Theresa had often thought that the Dower House, which was a fine example of Queen Anne architecture, was far lovelier than the Big House, which was a mansion of grey stone erected on the site of an earlier house by her great-grandfather.

It was huge and ponderous and, even when run by an army of servants, uncomfortable.

The Dower House always seemed to be filled with light and laughter when she and her mother were together.

But only she knew how miserable and unhappy her mother had been when her husband finally left her, and how the dark lines under her eyes in the morning made Theresa know she had cried all night.

Her mother tried hard not to show how miserable she was or how much she missed the man she loved.

Only when Theresa was much older, in fact just before her mother died, had she spoken to her confidentially and she understood much that had mystified her before.

"Your father married me because I was very rich," her mother had said. "I did not realise it at the time, but because he was so handsome and dashing I fell head-over-heels in love with him.'

She drew in her breath before she went on:

"Oh, my precious, be very careful to whom you give your heart. To a woman it is an agony beyond words to love while knowing one's love is not returned."

There was so much pain in her mother's voice that Theresa had clasped her fingers together until the knuckles showed white.

But she did not say anything, and her mother had continued:

"Be very, very careful to be certain that you are loved for yourself before you agree to marry any man, however charming, however persuasive. Money can be a joy, or a curse!"

She was silent for a moment before she went on in a low voice:

"And yet, if I had my time over again, I would feel that even the short time your father appeared to love me and we were happy together was worth all the suffering which came afterwards."

There were a thousand questions Theresa wanted to ask her mother, but she knew that the moment of confidence had passed, and it would be a mistake to press for more.

But gradually it all came together like the pieces of a jig-saw puzzle, and many of the things that had seemed incomprehensible when she was a child began to make sense.

She had to rely on little bits of information dropped by her relations, on what she herself remembered from years past, and of course inevitably the gossip of the older servants who found it impossible to keep their feelings to themselves.

"It's a cryin' shame, that's wot it is, the way Her Ladyship's been treated."

" 'andsome is as 'andsome does is wot I always says, and His Lordship's downfall be 'is looks. No woman can resist 'im!"

There were dozens of other such remarks which remained in Theresa's memory until she had been old enough to realise that her father's philanderings with other women had started soon after he and her mother were married.

First came his mysterious visits to London which he referred to as 'business affairs' then there were his journeys to Paris.

It was several years afterwards before Theresa heard his visits there described as 'an orgy of extravagance with the most expensive Charmers'.

She did not then know what that meant.

But soon, as the scandal of what was happening in the gayest City in the world percolated through to England, she heard about the beautiful women who attracted wealthy gentlemen from all over Europe and forced them to lay their fortunes at their feet.

At first what they said about her father was only a whisper when it seemed to Theresa playing with her toys, and later reading her books in a corner of the Drawing-Room that the conversation invariably got round to Paris and what was happening there.

"Of course with the Emperor giving a lead, what can you expect anybody else to do but follow him?" was one remark, and another:

"It is said that La Priva who is the most expensive of them all, wears two million pounds worth of jewellery!"

Theresa could not understand exactly what was meant by 'the most expensive', but when her father returned from Paris the first time she had heard her mother crying bitterly and saying as she did so:

"Why should you take my money to spend on those creatures? They would not be allowed to flaunt themselves in any civilised society!"

She had not heard any more, but the next time her father went to Paris her mother did not cry but only walked about the house with a pale face and tight lips.

Theresa was therefore aware that her father had once again taken a large sum of money to pay for his extravagances.

Now as she thought of what her mother had suffered over the years, Theresa looked down at the grave and said very quietly:

"I will never marry!"

It was a vow and she knew she would keep it. Never would she allow herself to be humiliated and suffer the agony her mother had suffered.

Things had got very much worse in the last few years when her father was seldom at home.

There was a woman in London who attracted him very much and despite the whisperings and gossip it was a long time before Theresa learnt that the lady in question was the wife of one of the most distinguished men at Court.

That her father was in love was to her unmistakable.

When he came home and she now guessed it was only because he needed more money – there was a dashing, raffish look about him.

There was also a light in his eyes which she was old enough to be aware denoted an excitement like a lion in pursuit of his prey.

She did not understand what it really meant because she was so innocent, but there was something aggressively masculine about him.

Although she disapproved of the way he treated her mother, she found it impossible not to admire him and not to enjoy the bitter-sweet fact that he was there with them.

"Do not go away, Papa," she pleaded the last time she had seen him. "Stay with us! I want to ride with you, and when you talk to me it is very exciting for me."

Her father had looked at her and said:

"You are growing up, Theresa, and very soon you will be a beautiful young woman."

It was as if he had only just realised it for himself, and Theresa answered:

"That is why it is so important for you to be with me, Papa."

"I wish I could, my dear," he had answered, "but I am not the right person to sponsor a *débutante* as your mother will tell you, and a great many other people as well!"

He spoke with a note of regret in his voice, but then his eyes brightened again as he said:

"We all have our own lives to lead and you will find that you have to lead yours. Do not let people impose on you, but be yourself."

"I want to do that, Papa," Theresa replied, "but there is so much for me to learn, and Mama and I are very quiet here."

Her father looked around the Drawing-Room and said in a voice that Theresa did not understand:

"It is too small, too restricting. I have always disliked being a big fish in a small pool. I want to be out in the open sea, doing what I want to do in my own way."

He spoke violently.

Then as if he knew Theresa was looking at him with a puzzled expression in her large eyes he said:

"Forget me, dearest child. I am no good to you, and you will be better off without me."

"Oh, no, Papa!"

He had kissed her, then driven away in a new Phaeton in which he had come down from London.

His hat was at an angle and he looked so smart and at the same time so raffish that she could understand the old Butler shaking his head as he watched him disappearing down the drive.

"His Lordship were always a lad!" he said as if he spoke to himself.

Theresa had gone to find her mother, but she was not in

the Drawing-Room and she guessed she had gone to her bedroom to lock herself in and cry despairingly.

That was the truth, and it was only some weeks later that her mother admitted that her father had left them for ever.

"Do you mean to say, Mama, that he is never coming back?" Theresa asked. "How can he do such a thing?"

"He has gone to live in France," her mother replied in a hard voice that seemed to be torn from her lips. "He has found somebody rich enough to look after him so that he no longer needs me, and I doubt if we shall ever see him again."

"Oh . . Mama!"

Tears had come into Theresa's eyes and while she fought for control she heard her mother say as if she spoke to herself:

"It is the women who are left behind who suffer."

After that she had refused to mention her father again, and although Theresa hoped he would write to her there was never a letter for her, or a present even at Christmas.

She did however hear snatches of information about him from various relatives who called to see them more out of curiosity, she thought, than because they wished to help her mother.

"I hear they go everywhere with the Prince Napoleon, and even the Emperor himself when the Empress is not present! Can you imagine our dear Queen sanctioning such outrageous behaviour?"

A year later Theresa had just come into the Drawing-Room as somebody was saying:

"It is true! She has left him! But he is consoling himself with one of the most flamboyant and notorious Courtesans in the whole of Paris. He gives parties for her which, it is said, exceed the orgies of the Romans! Where can he possibly find the money?"

Then they had seen Theresa coming through the doorway and had said no more.

Then six months ago the news arrived like a bombshell

from the family Solicitors that her father, the Earl of Denholme, had died in Paris.

There was nothing dramatic about it like fighting a duel. He had merely contracted a fever that had apparently swept through the Capital taking toll of an inordinate number of victims and among them her father.

His body had been brought back and buried in the family vault in the Church in the Park.

It was then for the first time that Theresa was aware of how many relatives she had, and how, disapproving of her father, they had deliberately ignored her mother and her all these years.

There were crowds of them and they were very unprepossessing, the majority elderly. In a way she could understand why her father had found them dull and refused to be restricted by their disapproval.

She resented the way they spoke of her as a 'poor child' because she was her father's daughter, and they obviously thought it was extremely regrettable that she was so attractive.

She could almost hear them whispering amongst themselves that she would undoubtedly get into trouble, having her father's blood in her.

What she could not excuse in them was their behaviour towards her mother who up until her dying day, was still very beautiful.

It was then she understood that her mother was regarded with a certain amount of suspicion and disapproval by her Holme In-Laws because she had French blood in her.

It seemed ridiculous, but already Theresa was learning that punishment for sinners was inflicted upon the innocent also if they were connected with them.

Her grandmother, her mother's mother had been in her own right the *Comtesse* de Chaufour.

She had married Theresa's grandfather because she loved him and not because it was an arranged marriage, as was usual in France.

They had met when her grandfather, Lord Greystone, was for a short time, Ambassador in Paris.

He was a widower and her mother had often told Theresa how the moment he had seen the young *Comtesse* he had fallen madly in love with her, and she with him.

Her mother's family were already negotiating for her to become engaged to an eligible young Frenchman whose lands in the Loire Valley marched with those of the Chaufours.

"But it was difficult to find any reasonable objection to her marrying my father, except that he was sixteen years older than she was," her mother had said, "but I have never known two people so happy."

There was a sad note in her mother's voice and a look in her eyes which had told Theresa that that was the happiness she had hoped she would find with her father only to be bitterly disillusioned.

Lord Greystone had died before his daughter had grown up and because he had no other children she had inherited a very large fortune.

"Yes, I became very rich," her mother told Theresa.

The way she spoke made her daughter aware that it had in fact, brought her nothing but unhappiness.

Only as Theresa walked back from the Churchyard did it occur to her that as she had no brothers or sisters everything her mother possessed was now hers.

She had been so unhappy when her mother died that she could only think of her loneliness.

Now she wondered what the money would mean to her, and once again she told herself she would never marry and no man should treat her as her mother had been treated by her father.

The doctors said that the Countess of Denholme had died because of a malignant growth which had given her a great deal of pain for some time before she admitted it.

Theresa did not believe them and was quite certain that when her father had died last autumn her mother now had no hope that he would ever return to her and had no wish to go on living.

It was as if she could see her fading away day by day,

growing weaker and weaker and less interested in anything. She obviously had no further wish to hold onto life and had finally let go.

"That is what happened," Theresa told herself, "because nobody ever mattered to her except Papa."

It was then that something hard and resolute seemed to grow up inside her as if it had suddenly matured and become part of her make-up.

"I will never suffer as Mama has!" she said aloud as she walked back through the Park under the oak-trees. "I will never let a man take my heart and trample on it, and I will never trust a man, however handsome or attractive he may be!"

She was thinking of her father and of the irresistible glint in his eye and the aura of excitement about him because he was going back to another woman.

"He was horrible, cruel, evil!" Theresa cried. "I hate Papa and I hate all men!"

She was so deep in her thoughts that as she went down the short drive to the front door of the Dower House she did not at first see the Phaeton outside it.

When she did so she was sure it belonged to her Uncle.

She had seen him at the Funeral and as he was escorted to the front pew as the new Earl of Denholme she knew he had a slight resemblance to her father.

He was not as handsome, nor so tall, and he had not the thin, elegant figure which had been part of her father's attraction.

He was much more heavily built and although he could not yet be forty-five, her Uncle was already going bald.

He had spoken to her after they had left the grave-side and said:

"I shall be moving into the family house, Theresa, as soon as possible and will of course come to call upon you."

Because she was trying to control her tears and was determined not to allow herself to be over-emotional in public, Theresa had only nodded an acknowledgement.

Now surprisingly her Uncle had called earlier than

expected and she told herself it would be a mistake, as he was now head of the family, not to be pleasant to him.

She therefore walked into the hall to find the old Butler who had come with them from the Big House waiting for her.

"His Lordship's in the Drawing-Room, M'Lady," he said.

"Is he alone?" Theresa asked.

"Yes, M'Lady."

Theresa did not ask any more questions, but walked into the Drawing-Room.

All the things in it were what her mother had treasured most, some of them being delightful pieces of inlaid furniture that she had brought from Paris after her own parents were dead.

There were also a few valuable French pictures which, filled with colour and light, were very different from the heavy family portraits which covered the walls of the Big House.

Her Uncle was standing in front of the fireplace in which there was a small fire burning, and as Theresa walked down the room towards him she thought he looked at her apprais-ingly, rather like a man inspecting a young horse he intended to buy.

She reached him and curtsied.

"Good-morning, Uncle Edward! I was not expecting you so soon."

"I am not moving into the house for another week or so," the Earl replied. "I just wished to have a meeting with the Estate Manager and I thought while I was here I would have a talk with you, Theresa."

"That was very kind of you, Uncle Edward. May I offer you some refreshment?"

"I have already told your servant to bring me a glass of claret," the Earl replied.

He looked round the room, his eyes resting on the French furniture and one of the Fragonard pictures.

"I see you have made yourselves very comfortable here. I

think it was sensible of your mother to move from the Big House which was far too large for the two of you.''

Theresa thought he almost added: ''After your father left,'' then prevented himself from doing so at the last moment.

''That is what we thought,'' she replied and sat down on the sofa.

''All the same,'' the Earl went on, ''you realise you cannot stay here alone now that your mother is dead.''

''I have thought of that,'' Theresa said quickly, ''and I intend to ask one of my Governesses, a Miss Robinson of whom I was very fond, to come and stay here with me.''

''That is sensible of you,'' the Earl approved. ''At the same time at your age – eighteen – you should be presented at Court and do the Season.''

''That is something I have no wish to do,'' Theresa replied quickly, ''and anyway I am of course, in mourning.''

''I am aware of that,'' the Earl said a little testily, ''but you will not preclude any festivities during the summer and by the autumn you will be nineteen. I therefore have a suggestion to put to you.''

Theresa thought she could guess what was coming and stiffened.

She had no wish to be introduced to the Social World which her father had once described as 'a marriage market' and in which she knew she would be labelled 'A desirable Heiress'.

She had already planned in her mind that she would travel perhaps with Miss Robinson, if she would agree to accompany her, or else with some other suitable chaperon.

She had a great wish to see Greece, and perhaps Egypt.

She thought it would be a great mistake however to suggest anything so adventurous to her Uncle and she only waited for what he had to say, being quite determined to resist it.

''I think you are aware,'' the Earl said rather heavily, ''that now both your father and mother are dead I, as head of the family, am your Guardian, and as your Guardian I am, after some considerable thought, convinced that the best thing for you is to be married as soon as possible!"

If the Earl had thrown a bomb at her Theresa could not have been more astonished.

"Did you say . . married . . Uncle Edward?"

"That is what I said, and that is what I meant!" the Earl replied. "You are a pretty girl and you have, as I understand after consulting with your mother's firm of Solicitors this morning, a very large fortune. This means, and you must be sensible enough to realise it, that you will be pursued by fortune-hunters who will want not you, but your money!"

Theresa had the uncomfortable feeling that he was thinking of her father before he went on:

"I have therefore as your Guardian chosen a husband who I think will meet with your approval and who certainly meets with mine."

"You have . . chosen a . . husband for . . me!" Theresa repeated incredulously.

"I do not think you have met my son," the Earl went on, "but you will find him a charming young man, intelligent, a good sportsman, and it is naturally important that he should marry as he will one day inherit my title."

The Earl paused before he continued:

"I will arrange for you to meet each other and, if you both agree, I see no reason, as long as you have a quiet marriage, why it should not take place in the summer."

Theresa was so astonished by what he was saying that she could for the moment, hardly credit that it was not part of her imagination.

And yet he was actually saying in his dry, crisp voice that she was to marry a man she had never seen simply because she had a large fortune.

Her first impulse was to say that she would never in any circumstances agree to such a proposal, and that anyway she had no intention of marrying any man, least of all a member of her own family.

However, Theresa was very intelligent and she realised that to antagonise her Uncle who she had to accept was her legal Guardian would be a great mistake.

She therefore held herself under control in a way that would have pleased her mother. She merely looked down so that he would not see the anger in her eyes and said quietly:

"You have surprised me, Uncle Edward! I did not expect you to suggest anything like that!"

"When you think it over you will realise that I have your best interests at heart," her Uncle answered, "and it is in fact, the sensible thing to do. You and Rupert can live in this house which means you will both be able to enjoy all the amenities of the estate, and of course your Aunt and I will be near at hand to look after you and guide you both."

Theresa had met her Aunt also at the Funeral and had known from the way she spoke of her mother that her disapproval of her father had extended to his wife, and doubtless to his daughter.

She knew now she had taken a dislike to the woman who was her Aunt Alice and she could not imagine that the eldest son of such a father and mother could have anything particularly attractive about him.

"What we ought to do," the Earl said, laying down the law in what Theresa was certain was his habitually abrupt manner, "is to send for Miss Robinson, if that is her name, and she can stay here with you until we have everything in order up at the house."

He paused as if thinking it over, then continued:

"Then you can come to us, and we will look after you until your marriage. Your Aunt will help you with your trousseau, and, as I say, as long as it is a quiet family affair it can take place perhaps at the end of June or the beginning of July. There is no point in having a long engagement."

Theresa knew as he spoke that his real reason for thinking so was that he was afraid she might get off the hook and escape from what might be a desirable marriage from his point of view, but from hers would be a hell she had no intention of entering.

The way her father had behaved towards her mother had made her suspicious of all men and she was also very sensitive of physical contact with other people.

To imagine being forced into intimacy with a man she had never even met, whatever he might be like, was so appalling that she felt like screaming at the Earl that he was insane to think of such an idea.

Then she was aware that this would gain her nothing. He would despise her, as she was certain he had despised her father, and could be more determined than he was already to get his own way.

"I must be clever about this," Theresa told herself.

After a moment she said:

"It is very kind of you to think of me and be so concerned for my welfare, Uncle Edward, but I would be very grateful if I could have just a little time to adjust myself to losing my mother and of course my father in such a short space of time."

"That is understandable," the Earl agreed. "Of course you can stay here with Miss Robinson for some weeks. It will take us that time at any rate, to get the house in order and make a few alterations and that sort of thing."

"Yes, of course!" Theresa agreed.

"Well, that is settled," he said.

As he spoke the door opened and the old Butler came in carrying a silver tray on which there was a glass and a bottle of the best claret which Theresa knew he had had to fetch from the cellar.

He set the tray down on a side-table, poured the claret into the glass and offered it to the Earl.

He took a sip and smacked his lips and said:

"Good, very good! I expect your father chose this."

"Papa put down a lot of good wines for them to mature," Theresa said.

"Very sensible indeed!" the Earl approved. "Rupert, like all young men, has to learn a great deal about wine before he can become a connoisseur. But he will learn, you can be sure of that."

There was so much satisfaction in his voice that Theresa knew her Uncle was looking forward to drinking a lot of the wine himself.

It made her dislike of him increase until it was hard to speak respectfully.

Aloud she said:

"I am glad it meets with your approval, Uncle Edward."

The Earl finished the glass, then as the Butler left the room and they were alone he said:

"Your mother's Solicitor – what is his name? Mayhew? – is coming to see you in the morning. I told him it was unnecessary as I had seen the Will, but he insisted you should know exactly what your mother left you."

"I would like to know that."

Theresa was quite certain it was a very large sum, which was why her Uncle would have preferred to keep her in ignorance.

Then he went on:

"I will of course advise you in the future, and help you and guide you as to what you can and cannot spend. There is no point in your being extravagant like your poor father. But you will certainly not lack a penny or two."

He laughed as if it was a joke and when he had finished his glass of claret he said:

"You are a lucky young woman, but do not let that go to your head. Just realise you are also lucky to have a family behind you who will not let you make mistakes and get into the hands of the wrong sort of people."

Theresa knew that meant fortune-hunters who would marry her for her money, which was exactly what his son intended to do.

She rose to her feet and said quietly:

"Thank you for coming to see me, Uncle Edward, and for all the plans you have been making on my behalf. I will send a carriage for Miss Robinson this afternoon. She lives only about fifteen miles away. I think when she attended Mama's Funeral she was aware that I would be grateful if she would stay here with me."

"Good! Good!" the Earl said. "And do not forget – as soon as your Aunt has everything arranged at the house and enough servants to make sure of our comfort, you will come to us and be part of our family, which you will in fact be as soon as you are married.''

''Thank you, Uncle Edward.''

He patted her on the shoulder, then walked towards the door with Theresa following him.

He crossed the hall and went down the steps to where his Phaeton was waiting. It was a rather old-fashioned and heavy vehicle.

He climbed into it and then, as if he was aware of what she was thinking, the Earl said:

''I must indulge myself when I arrive here by buying some new carriages and certainly a new Phaeton for myself, and I expect the stables are almost empty.''

He did not wait for her reply but picked up the reins before he said:

''Goodbye, Theresa. Look after yourself!''

He drove off and as she watched him go Theresa thought that was exactly what she would do.

She would look after herself, and that meant not doing any of the things her Uncle had planned for her.

Now he had gone she found herself shaking with fury at the way he had mapped out her life without so much as consulting her, without even considering that she might have some feelings in the matter.

She walked across the hall and into the Drawing-Room, knowing that she had to be alone. She had to think.

Then as she looked around the room which her mother had made so comfortable she felt that her whole being was calling out a question and it seemed to be ringing in her ears.

''What am I to do? Oh, God, what am I to do?''

As if she was caught in a trap which was closing on her, she saw herself being taken away from the house where she had been happy with her mother to the big gaunt family mansion on the other side of the Park.

Once there, there would be no escape and she would be forced, because there was no alternative, to marry her cousin simply because not only he but his father wanted her money.

Nobody knew better than she did that the reason why they had left the Big House in the first place was that it was so extremely expensive to run and with the cost of maintaining the estate, as well, even her mother's huge fortune had felt the strain.

In any case, after her father left them her mother had hated the house and had been very much happier in the beautiful Queen Anne Dower House.

Now Theresa reasoned, her Uncle had every intention of taking up his position as head of the family in the ancestral mansion.

But he could not maintain it any more than her father had been able to do without a fortune to draw on.

He had therefore concocted this idea which she could see from his point of view was a very sensible one, and if she married his eldest son Rupert they could live in great comfort.

But no thought had been given to the fact that Rupert did not love her and it was therefore more than likely that he too would behave in the way in which her father had behaved towards her mother.

He would first go to London on short expeditions, then perhaps he too would find Paris irresistible.

"I would rather die than endure that," Theresa told herself, "and even if I were not in love with him as Mama was in love with Papa, it would still be a humiliation and a degradation to be left at home with everybody including the servants being sorry for me!"

Once again the question was there ringing in her ears.

"What am I to do?"

She knew the answer quite clearly.

She had to go away and where she went or how did not really matter, but she would go away and make a life of her own.

But she would certainly have to be clever about it.

She was quite certain that her Uncle would not give in easily.

He had everything planned, everything mapped out in his

own mind, and her fortune would not escape him if he could help it.

Theresa drew in her breath.

Then for the moment looking older than she was with her grey eyes very serious she sat down on the window-seat to stare out into the sunlit garden.

Chapter Two

HAVING SAT thinking for a long time, Theresa walked slowly up the stairs and along the passage to the Sewing-Room where she knew she would find Genevieve.

Now over fifty, Genevieve had come from France with her mother when she married to look after her and love her ever since Theresa could remember.

She had now been in England for so long that even the servants had forgotten that she was French and called her 'Gennie'!

It was in fact the name that Theresa had given her when she was very tiny, being unable to pronounce 'Genevieve'.

She was, as Theresa had expected, sitting at the square deal table in the centre of the Sewing-Room mending the lace on one of her nightgowns and so intent on what she was doing that she did not at first hear her come into the room.

Then when she looked up and saw Theresa she smiled.

It was a kindly smile in a kind face, but Genevieve's eyes

were worried, and as Theresa walked to the table and sat down on the other side of it, she asked:

"What did your Uncle want, M'Lady?"

Theresa drew in her breath.

"He told me I am to marry his son Rupert, to save me from fortune-hunters, he said. But it is really because they need my fortune!"

Gennie's hands dropped into her lap.

"It's not possible!" she exclaimed.

There was only the faintest French accent in the way she spoke, and there was no doubt she was horrified at what she had heard.

She stared at Theresa as if she must have been mistaken.

"It is true!" Theresa said. "And now, Gennie, you have to help me."

"How can I do that?"

"I have to go away, to hide somewhere! As you are well aware, after the way Papa treated Mama, I loathe all men!"

"You'll change your mind, *ma petite*," Gennie said consolingly, "but they must give you time."

"Uncle Edward has no intention of giving me time," Theresa replied sharply. "He is already arranging my marriage for the end of June or the beginning of July!"

"Mon Dieu!"

The words were very quiet, but Theresa knew how shocked the old maid was not only that she should be married, but that the time for mourning her beloved mother should be so short.

"That is why I have to escape from here as quickly as possible," Theresa went on quietly, "and the only person I can ask to help me, Gennie, is you!"

"You know I'd do anything you want," Gennie replied, "but you're too young, M'Lady, to be on your own. You must hide with one of your relations."

"Do you suppose any of them would shelter me against Uncle Edward's wishes?" Theresa asked. "Besides, they would be pleased that Mama's money was to be kept in the family."

Gennie nodded her head as if she understood, and Theresa was sure she was aware how much her mother's money was needed by the Earl if he was to live in the Family mansion and keep up any sort of style.

Because she could not sit still Theresa rose from the table to walk across the room saying:

"Mama suffered all her life because she was rich, and apart from my own revulsion at being married off to a man I have never seen, I would do anything to prevent the Holme family from spending my money without even consulting me."

Her voice deepened and grew a little louder as she said:

"The only reason why Papa ever came home towards the end of his life was that he wanted more of Mama's money. My relations were not interested in how lonely Mama and I were until she died. Now they are concerning themselves with me simply because I am rich!"

She walked to the window fighting the tears that had come to her eyes – tears of sorrow aroused by speaking of her mother, but also tears of anger.

If she had behaved as she wanted to, she would have stamped and screamed and even thrown things about.

But the self-control she had been taught to exercise ever since she was small made her stand looking out onto the sunshine, struggling not to speak the words that came to her lips.

After what seemed a long time she turned and walked back to the table saying as she did so:

"Let us make plans, Gennie."

"What can we do, M'Lady?" Gennie asked. "Besides if you run away from your Uncle he'll prevent you from having any money."

"I have thought of that already," Theresa replied, "and that is why we have to take as much as we can with us, and also earn enough to keep us in some sort of comfort."

"Earn?" Gennie almost screeched the word. "How can you earn money? You – a lady, who has never worked in her life!"

"That is true," Theresa agreed, "and yet with the very extensive education which Mama insisted on my having there must be something I can do!"

She sat down cupping her small pointed chin in her hands.

"Now let us be sensible, Gennie," she said, "and think what talents I have."

She paused before she began slowly:

"First, I speak perfect French, Mama saw to that! Secondly, I can sew – not as well as you – but well. Thirdly, I can ride better than most women, and very nearly as well as Papa. Fourthly . . . "

She paused.

"There must be something else I can do which will earn money!"

As she spoke she looked at Gennie who was still staring at her in bewilderment.

"Are you really telling me, M'Lady, that you intend to earn your living in any of these ways? *C'est impossible!*"

"No, it is not impossible!" Theresa said firmly, "and frankly, as I have no intention of having a husband or children to look after I must occupy myself, otherwise my mind will become atrophied."

She could see that Gennie did not understand the word and she added:

"Paralysed, wasted away, starved, degenerate, stupid like that of most of my relations and the young women of the Social World who Papa used to say never had a thought in their heads except of chasing a man in the 'Marriage Market'."

As she spoke she thought that her father had thought of little else but chasing after women.

Because it made her angry to think of him she went on quickly:

"I should enjoy having something to do, especially if it meant that you and I could live in some comfort, even if we cannot rely on my fortune."

"It's wrong, unnatural!" Gennie said positively. "You must speak to His Lordship, and tell him you cannot do what he wants. And anyway, you're in mourning for your dear mother for at least a year!"

"Now listen, Gennie," Theresa said firmly, "then we need argue about it no more. By the laws of England Uncle Edward is my Guardian, and a Guardian can force his Ward to do anything he wishes, in this case to marry my Cousin Rupert and live here in this house as his wife."

She knew that Gennie being French was not as revolted by the idea of an arranged marriage as she was and she added quickly:

"I made a vow never to marry any man who only wanted me because I was rich, and if you will not come away with me, Gennie, then I have to go alone."

The maid gave a cry of horror.

"*No, non,* that is something that mustn't happen! You wouldn't be safe. You're far too beautiful!"

"Then you will have to look after me," Theresa said, "so stop arguing, Gennie, and let us get down to the bare facts. What can I do?"

There was silence. Then Gennie gave a little cry.

"But of course, it's quite simple – you must go to Paris, to your relatives. You may not have seen them for some years, but I'm sure that like all French families the Chaufours would be loyal and would welcome you."

"I am sure they would for *Grandmère*'s sake as well as Mama's," Theresa replied, "but when Uncle Edward finds me missing, that is one of the first places he is likely to look for me."

"You mean he'd bring you back?"

"The Law would support him and nothing the French could say would stop him!"

Gennie sighed.

"It's not right!"

She looked wistful as she spoke and Theresa knew that she had always longed to go back to France.

But because France was where her father went, her mother, even when she was alone and unhappy, had never made any attempt after the death of her father and mother, the *Comte* and *Comtesse* de Chaufour, to visit her other relatives."

"If only *Grandmère* were alive," Theresa said softly, "I am sure she would hide me and defy Uncle Edward to discover where I was."

Gennie gave a little laugh.

"*Madame la Comtesse* was always brave, and there was never anybody in trouble whom she would not help."

Her words conjured up for Theresa a vision of the *Comtesse* when she had last seen her.

She had been very beautiful even in old age, with her white hair exquisitely arranged, her skin translucent despite the lines round her eyes. These still sparkled and still softened with love when she spoke of her daughter and reminisced about the happiness she had enjoyed with her husband.

After Lord Greystone had died she had gone back to live in France with her own family and called herself by her own name.

Her marriage to an Englishman had not changed her and everything about her was still French – her beauty her *chic*, her outlook, and above all, her warm and emotional temperament.

It made her unpredictable and at the same time so fascinating that it was impossible for any man or woman who knew her not to love her.

"Yes, *Grandmère* would understand," Theresa said, following her own thoughts.

"I remember when she cooked here how she used to make us laugh," Gennie said, "and when she first taught you to cook when you were very small you used to laugh so much that the kitchen walls would echo with the sound!"

As she finished speaking, Theresa gave a little cry.

"To cook!' she exclaimed. 'Gennie, that is what I can do! I can cook!"

Gennie stared at her as she went on:

"Everybody needs good food! You remember the last time *Grandmère* came to stay how you and I cooked the dishes she had taught me, and she said how good they were."

"I remember how disagreeable Cook was about it," Gennie said. "She sulked for days because she considered herself insulted."

"*Grandmère* would never have eaten English dishes which Papa liked and which Mama tolerated only for his sake."

Then in a different voice Theresa continued:

"But of course, I can cook as well as, if not better than *Grandmère* who often said herself that if she was penniless she would have a Restaurant of her own, and it would be the success of Paris."

Gennie was still staring at Theresa as if trying to understand what she was saying, and she went on:

"Now listen, Gennie, I cannot afford to start a Restaurant straight away, but that is something you and I will do in the future. First I shall take a place as a Chef in some distinguished private house where we shall be comfortable, and which would be the last place Uncle Edward would think of looking for me."

"You can't do such a thing, M'Lady. It's impossible!" Gennie said firmly.

"Why should it be?" Theresa argued. "I cook superbly, and you can help me, as you have helped me in the past. Anyway, if I am in the kitchen, I shall certainly not be pursued by fortune-hunters!"

Gennie looked at her and thought she would be pursued by men whether she had money or not.

She did not say so, but only retorted:

"You're not going to become a servant, M'Lady! So it's no use your talking such nonsense!"

"It is not nonsense, and it is what I am going to do!" Theresa answered. "Cooking in England would be no use where people only want roast beef and apple-pie. We shall have to go to France, and actually as you are French and I have French blood in me, I am quite certain we shall settle down and be very happy there."

"Settle down?"

Gennie's voice rose almost to a shriek.

"Are you intending, M'Lady, to spend your life slaving

away as a menial instead of taking your proper place as a Lady of Quality?''

''As a Lady of Quality,'' Theresa snapped, ''or rather, a Lady with a fortune, I shall be married in four months time to a man I have never even seen, a man who has no interest in me, and merely wants to get his greedy hands into my pocket.''

She spoke so savagely that the maid moved backwards as if she was almost afraid of her violence.

Then as if she knew how serious Theresa was she said pleadingly:

''*Ma petite*, this is not something you should do. What would your dear Mother say? God rest her soul.''

''Mama would tell me not to marry Cousin Rupert.''

There was silence. Then Gennie said:

''Let us go to France, if His Lordship does not prevent it. But when you get there, you'll find one of your French relations and ask them to hide you.''

''And suppose they refuse?'' Theresa asked. ''What do we do then? Come back here with no chance of being able to escape another time? No, Gennie, if we go, we start a new life, and I have the feeling that we will make a success of it.''

She smiled and put out her hands across the table.

''Come with me, Gennie dear. Look after me, take care of me, as you have always done. Although you may not believe it, I am quite sure Mama would approve.''

She saw the tears come into the old maid's eyes and there was no need for more words as she knew she had won.

******

The following morning Mr. Mayhew arrived to see Theresa.

She was waiting for him and had already planned exactly what she would say.

She received him in the Drawing-Room and after she had asked him whether he would prefer coffee or a glass of wine as a refreshment after his journey, they settled down to business.

"Your mother's Will was quite simple, Lady Theresa," Mr. Mayhew began. "She has left you everything she possessed with the condition that you use only the income from the money during your lifetime, and the capital is entailed onto your children."

"And if I do not have any children?"

"Then the money is to be distributed amongst the Chaufour family in France."

This confirmed Theresa's idea that her mother had never liked her Holme-In-Laws, although she had never said so.

"There are however a few exceptions," Mr. Mayhew continued. "If at any time you wish to buy a house, then you can draw the money out of the capital fund, and if at any time you require a Trust Fund for your children for their education, marriage or anything like that, then the same applies."

He paused to say with a faint smile:

"I think however, as your mother was exceedingly rich you will find the income, which is a very large one, enough for all your needs, however expensive they may be."

Theresa was aware that her mother was making sure that any husband she had could not, as her father had done, extract large sums from her.

At the same time, she was thinking that her idea of running a Restaurant was not as impossible as it had at first appeared.

That would certainly count as a house, and once she was free of her Uncle's insistence that she should marry her Cousin Rupert, she could set herself up in business as she wished to do.

She knew however that it was something she could not say to Mr. Mayhew who would be horrified at the idea and would doubtless immediately go to her Uncle and tell him what she had suggested.

Instead she said meekly:

"I am sure Mama was doing what she thought was best for me, and I am very grateful."

"You can certainly have everything material you want in

life," Mr. Mayhew said, "and your mother has listed a number of her employees to whom she has left legacies and has said that you can add to that list anybody whom you feel she has omitted."

Theresa took the list from him and read it, realising that her mother had been very generous to all the servants and especially, as she would have expected, to Genevieve.

Reading through it carefully she said:

"There are one or two more people who I think should have an appropriate sum of money. I am also going to ask you, Mr. Mayhew for quite a large sum for myself, as I must go to London to buy myself some mourning clothes."

"Of course, Lady Theresa," Mr. Mayhew agreed. "You have only to tell me what you require."

"I shall need £500 for the legacies," Theresa said speaking quickly, "and another £500 for my clothes."

"Surely it would be more convenient, Lady Theresa," Mr. Mayhew said, "to have the accounts sent to me, and I can pay them."

Theresa smiled.

"I agree that would be a good idea," she replied, "but you know how seldom Mama and I have been away from here in the last three years. Since therefore I am not known in the shops in London, I doubt if they would give me credit without a great deal of explanation. So it would be much easier to pay cash."

"I see your point," Mr. Mayhew said, "but I do not like the idea of your wandering about with so much money on your person."

"If you are worrying," Theresa said, "then I have another suggestion."

She had in fact, just thought of it herself.

"I could easily open a Bank Account in London, as I expect I shall be going there quite often in the future. Will you please arrange to deposit £5,000 in a Bank as near as possible to where I shall be staying as soon as you can? I can then draw cheques as and when I require them."

"Of course," Mr. Mayhew agreed, "and I should feel that

you are safer and not at the mercy of every pick-pocket or robber who roams the streets of London."

"I am sure you are needlessly apprehensive," Theresa replied. "However, if you would arrange that immediately I should be grateful, because I shall be travelling to London the day after tomorrow."

Mr. Mayhew put the papers back in his brief-case.

"I will arrange, My Lady, for one of my clerks to bring over the money you need for the legacies in the morning."

"Thank you," Theresa said. "You are very kind to take so much trouble."

"It was always a pleasure to look after your mother, Lady Theresa, and I hope you will trust me to look after your interests in the future."

The way he spoke made Theresa quite certain that he was aware of her Uncle's plans for her, and she knew that her Uncle dealt with a different firm of Solicitors.

"I promise you, Mr. Mayhew, I will always look to you for help and guidance, as Mama did."

She knew the Solicitor was pleased and had in fact been apprehensive at the thought of losing such a wealthy client.

Theresa paused for a moment. Then she said:

"There is one thing I would like to ask you, Mr. Mayhew."

"What is that?"

"That you keep whatever business we transact together confidential and secret."

"If that is what you wish, Lady Theresa, then of course I will agree."

"I do wish it, very sincerely," Theresa said. "To be honest, I was rather perturbed when I learnt from my Uncle that you had shown him the contents of my mother's Will before I had actually seen it myself."

Mr. Mayhew looked uncomfortable.

"I can only apologise, if in so doing I have offended Your Ladyship," he said, "but His Lordship was very insistent that he had a right, as your Guardian, to know exactly what your future prospects were."

"Does that mean in the future he can overrule my wishes, even though he does not employ your firm?"

As if Mr. Mayhew was suddenly aware of what Theresa was implying he said:

"I think I am right in stating, My Lady, that I can refuse to reveal to His Lordship anything that is confidential unless he obtains a Court Order on the ground that he is your Guardian."

He paused before he added:

"That course of action is in fact, lengthy, cumbersome and expensive."

Theresa smiled.

She felt quite certain that unless it was of great importance her Uncle would not press Mr. Mayhew to divulge anything she wished him not to know.

Anyway, he had now found out what really mattered – the extent of her fortune – and had decided on the best way to get it into his own hands.

She was, in fact, astounded by the amount of money her mother had left her.

It was such a large sum that it seemed incredible that her father could have spent the income so easily and quickly, returning so often for further large amounts of capital.

Then she remembered the women in Paris for whom men like her father gave orgies which rivalled those of the Romans and threw fortunes at their feet.

Once again she felt a surge of hatred rise up in her, but her voice was steady and her feelings did not show themselves in her face as she said:

"I am hoping, Mr. Mayhew, that there will be no unpleasantness about what I own. I am very thankful to know that I can turn to you if I am in any difficulty, and that anything I have to say will be a secret between us two."

"Of course, My Lady," Mr. Mayhew agreed, "and I am very honoured that you should trust me."

When Theresa saw him off at the front door she told herself she had been very clever.

She had now ensured that she had a large amount of

money with which to escape, and which would keep herself and Gennie in comfort for some time.

But she knew also that if they were really in trouble she could easily obtain some more money through Mr. Mayhew, even though it might be dangerous even for him to know where they were.

She had already reasoned that a certain escape from her Uncle's machinations could only come when Rupert had married somebody else.

If she was missing for three or four years, the Holmes' need of money might persuade him to find another heiress, in which case she could then, if she wished, return to England.

In the meantime, Mr. Mayhew would take care that her fortune accumulated, and it could not be touched by anybody else.

"Everything is working out exactly as I want it to!" Theresa said delightedly as she ran up the stairs to tell Gennie what had happened.

******

The next day a clerk from Mr. Mayhew's office brought Theresa the sum of £500.

With it came a letter warning her to be very careful with it, and to hand over the money to those to whom she wanted to give it as quickly as possible.

There were actually a few people who had come to work at the Dower House after her mother had made her Will, and Theresa gave them appropriate sums, ensuring they did not exceed those of the servants who had been there longer.

It was enough however to delight them and, she thought, ensure that they would not be penniless if they were dismissed by her Uncle when she could not be found.

She wrote a letter which she intended to post from London after she and Gennie had left.

In it she requested Mr. Mayhew to keep up the Dower House at her expense, while she was away and pay the wages of the servants who had been with them for so long, until further notice.

She did not explain why she was going away, or where she intended to be.

She knew he would hear about it sooner or later and being a shrewd man would guess her reasons for going into hiding.

However much she might trust Mr. Mayhew, she was afraid that her Uncle would by some means extract the information from him, if he had any idea that he knew of her whereabouts.

As the Earl of Denholme, her Uncle was now a very important person in the County, and even a well-established firm of Solicitors could suffer if he started a vendetta against them.

"I must not put Mr. Mayhew in that sort of position, unless things become very desperate," Theresa said.

She thought with satisfaction how much money she could draw out of the Bank in London after it had been deposited there.

The next day Gennie had packed almost everything she possessed besides a great number of her mother's clothes.

"We do not want to buy any more than is absolutely essential," Theresa said, "and I think, Gennie, it would be a mistake for me to be in deep mourning when we arrive in France."

The maid looked at her with startled eyes and she explained:

"It creates an impression of gloom which no one wants in an employee. Besides, if Uncle Edward suspects that I have gone to France and searches for me there, he will obviously ask if they have seen a young woman in deep mourning, and it might make his task that much easier."

"But it's disrespectful to your beloved mother!" Gennie objected.

"I loved Mama, and I will never love anybody else as much," Theresa replied. "At the same time I know she would understand, and certainly *Grandmère* would, that the most important thing at the moment is for us to escape from

Uncle Edward and the man he has chosen to become my husband."

"It's not right to suggest such a thing, the moment your mother is dead!" Gennie muttered.

"It makes little difference whether now or later," Theresa answered, "for I have no intention of ever marrying! Therefore the only thing I can do, as I told you, is to start a new life, and once we set foot in France, Gennie, I am going to be French!"

Gennie looked surprised and Thesesa continued:

"I have to choose myself a name. What do you suggest? Obviously it cannot be 'Chaufour'!"

Gennie thought for a moment. Then she said:

"It's difficult and I'll never remember not to say: 'M'Lady'!"

"I shall be very angry if you forget!" Theresa said. "Do you realise that if we are discovered and sent back it will mean that you will have to live at the Big House, which you have always hated, and eat great lumps of roast beef for the rest of your life!"

Gennie held up her hands in horror and Theresa laughed.

In the past when Theresa had cooked special dishes for her mother she knew that Gennie had always finished up anything that was left over, and had said:

"That's what I call food for a civilised person!"

Theresa had told her mother what Gennie had said and she replied:

"I am not surprised, dearest! The French, from the poorest peasant upwards, think of the preparation of food as an Art, and there is no doubt that where that is concerned they *are* the most civilised race in the whole of Europe!"

Theresa had been quite small when she had first been able to make a *soufflé* that was so light it could almost float away on the breeze.

Her grandmother had taught her to make *quenelles* of pike which melted in the mouth, and her *mille-feuilles* were fantastic.

She could also cook game so that the dish not only looked

a picture and appealed to the eye, but had a flavour that no English cook could achieve.

"Where did you learn to cook so well, *Grandmère*?" Theresa asked her once.

"I was one of a large family," the *Comtesse* replied, "and my father who was a great epicure always said that the way to a man's heart was through his stomach. He therefore made all his daughters learn from our Chef how to produce meals of which he approved, and he was very critical!"

"And when you married, Grandpapa enjoyed them?" Theresa enquired.

"Your grandfather was in the Diplomatic Service and spent more time abroad than in England. He ate the food of Greece, Turkey and some of the Eastern countries, but he always said it was an unspeakable joy to be in Paris. When he became Ambassador people flocked to the Embassy to eat."

Her grandmother laughed before she went on:

"You can imagine that when he retired I had to be certain that his meals were just as good as when we had a superlative Chef, and therefore I very often cooked for your grandfather and myself. In fact, I was so good that he began to insist that I did all the cooking, which left me very little time for anything else!"

She laughed again before she said:

"And you, my precious little one, are a natural cook, which means that just as a gardener has 'green fingers', you have the art of making everything you touch taste delicious!"

Theresa had been thrilled by what her grandmother had said at the time, and now she knew that what she had learnt was going to save her from a life of misery and humiliation.

"I shall have to be very clever about it," she thought, "otherwise Uncle Edward will guess what I am trying to do and prevent it."

******

Theresa and Gennie arrived in London and went to stay at

Holme House which had been closed for the last few years after her father had gone to live in France.

Before that it had been kept open entirely for him as her mother seldom went there.

It was a large, rather ugly mansion in Charles Street off Berkeley Square, and there were only a few old servants to care for it who had obviously grown lazy in the years when it had been so little occupied.

They were extremely apprehensive, Theresa found, now that her mother was dead, in case the new Earl should wish to dispense with their services.

"What'll become of us, M'Lady, if we can't stay here?" the old Butler enquired.

"Do you wish to stay?" Theresa asked gently.

"We'd like to retire, M'Lady, if it was possible, but we've nowhere to go an' no savings."

"No savings?"

"Our son's bin in a bit o' trouble, M'Lady, an' we've had to help him out."

Theresa did not ask any questions, but from other things the old couple said to her she learnt that their son was a ne'er-do-well who had extracted from them everything they possessed.

It made her hate men even more than she did already.

She sat down and wrote a letter to Mr. Mayhew instructing him to provide the old couple with a cottage on the estate and pay them a generous pension every week.

Then she added:

"Make quite certain that my Uncle does not turn them out, and if there is any trouble, buy their house for them so that it is theirs, and he cannot dispose of it."

She told the old couple what she had done and also gave them £100 which she said her mother had left them as a legacy.

They were overwhelmed with joy and she thought they would be sensible enough not to let their son know about it. At least it would make them feel secure.

There was a groom in the mews at the back who looked

after any horses that were stabled there when her father had stayed in London, and his wife cleaned in the house.

They were Cockneys and would never have been happy anywhere away from London.

They were however, comparatively young, so Theresa told them that if her uncle did not require them any longer they should apply to Mr. Mayhew who would look after them and see that they had their wages paid until they found other employment.

She was being extra careful over everybody because she was quite certain that when her uncle found that she was not available to marry Rupert he would have to make strict economies.

Because he was pompous and pleased to be in her father's shoes she was quite certain he would make every effort to live at the Big House as every Earl had done before him.

At the same time, it was almost an impossibility without plenty of money, and she knew only too well that the Holmes were all very hard up.

"You would have thought in the circumstances," she reasoned, "that they would have made every effort to pander to my mother, especially after Papa had left her and they must have known how unhappy she was."

Then she was aware it had been her French Mother's blood which had made them keep away, even though it was very much in their own interests to act differently.

"They are both cruel and despicable!" Theresa cried angrily. "I hate them as much as I hate Papa, and every male member of the family!"

She did not trouble when in London to visit any of the shops. Instead she merely went to the Bank to find out if the money she had asked for had been paid in.

She was too clever to draw it all out.

Instead she took out £3,000 which was a large enough sum to make the Manager ask her anxiously if she was wise to withdraw so much.

"Unfortunately," Theresa replied, "I have some outstanding debts to pay which have only just come to my notice, and which I prefer to deal with myself rather than ask the assistance of Mr. Mayhew."

She spoke in a manner which she knew would make the Manager think that they concerned her father, and he instantly agreed to give her the money in the large notes she demanded.

She carefully stowed some away in secret places in their luggage and the rest she gave to Gennie to wear in a belt next to her skin.

"I'm not having any greedy thieves feeling in my pocket!" the old maid said aggressively. "You've given me something for safe-keeping and safe I'll keep it, M'Lady!"

"I knew you would say that, Gennie," Theresa laughed. "I am therefore trusting more of it to you, so do not fall overboard when we cross the Channel or the fish will have a very expensive meal!"

She laughed at her own joke, but Gennie said seriously:

"The moment we reach Paris we'll put all this money into a Bank where it'll be safe, and not walk about asking for trouble."

"I am asking for nothing except that nobody should know who I am," Theresa replied, "and do not forget, I am *Mademoiselle* Beauvais, and we speak French and not English."

"I'll not forget!" Gennie said stoutly, and the moment they set foot on the cross-Channel steamer started to speak in her own language.

It was not until they actually docked at Calais that Theresa felt she could relax.

All the time they were travelling from Victoria she was nervous.

Supposing by some terrible stroke of bad luck she would be seen and recognised by some friend of her father's?

Supposing she met somebody whom she knew, who would immediately tell her Uncle that she was on her way to France?

She was hoping that he would be misled by the information she had left with the staff at Dower House.

"After I have bought some black gowns in London," she

told them, "I am taking Gennie with me to the North where I intend to stay with one of my friends. It will only be for a few weeks, but I feel I must get away."

They thought she was referring to the unhappiness of being in the house without her mother and they said sympathetically:

"That's a sensible idea, M'Lady. It'll do you good to see new faces and be with somebody of your own age."

"Look after everything until I come back," Theresa said, "and I will let you know when that will be."

The family carriage had taken her to London, changing horses on the way. They stayed the night, then left early the next morning.

She had told the old couple at Holme House the same story, and she knew her Uncle would check both places when he really began to wonder what had happened to her.

She hoped, unless something unforeseen should happen that she would have three or four weeks respite before he grew anxious.

That was why when she was quite certain there was nobody on the train or on the cross-Channel steamer whom she had ever seen before, she felt safe, and there was a wonderful feeling of freedom in the air when she reached Calais.

The train for Paris was waiting near the Quay, and she and Gennie got into a First Class Carriage.

Theresa had decided to travel First Class not only because it was more comfortable, but also because she thought they could be alone and she was still trying to decide what she should do as soon as she arrived in Paris.

Despite Gennie's reluctance to agree to the idea, she was still determined that she should start off by getting employment as a Chef.

"We have to be practical," she said to Gennie. "Our money will not last for ever, and although it seems a lot at the moment it is very easy for it to dwindle and dwindle until we shall be forced to ask Mr. Mayhew for more, and that might be dangerous."

"You can't work as a servant, M'Lady!"

"Mademoiselle!" Theresa corrected. "And if I am to be a servant, I shall at least be a very superior one. After all, Chefs, as you well know, are a law unto themselves. Mama often told me how grandly the Chef used to behave when she lived at home and how all the rest of the household were afraid of him."

"He was a *man, M'mselle!"*

"I will make them frightened of me!" Theresa replied. "Anyway, I will have my own way, you wait and see!"

She knew Gennie did not believe her, which only strengthened her determination to do what she wanted to do.

Before they had left for France she had forged the most glowing references on the writing-paper which was surmounted by the family crest.

One reference was supposedly from her mother the Countess of Denholme, the other from her grandmother the *Comtesse* Marie de Chaufour.

She knew because she looked so young that this might seem out of date.

She therefore explained in the letter from her grandmother that after her husband Lord Greystone, one-time British Ambassador to Paris had died, she had employed *Mademoiselle* Theresa Beauvais as her Chef, and found her a superlative cook, worthy of the finest traditions of French cuisine.

It was so elegant and so extravagantly complimentary that Theresa had laughed when she finished it.

"If that does not entitle me to be employed in the Tuilleries Palace by the Emperor," she said, "I shall be very surprised!"

"I've always heard that the food in the Tuilleries Palace is not good," Gennie replied. "The Empress Eugenie's Spanish and doesn't understand the French Palate."

"Then the Emperor should know better!" Theresa said firmly. "However I am sure that with these references every epicure in France will be willing to employ me!"

She did not realise that Gennie looked sceptical and gave a deep sigh.

She was in fact, quite sure that her mistress, being a woman, was going to find it very difficult to get employment as a Chef, and she was far more apprehensive about the future than she dared to express.

At the same time, knowing how young, innocent and inexperienced of the world Theresa was, she had no intention of allowing her to go anywhere without being there to look after her.

She had adored the Countess ever since she had first seen her and thought her the most beautiful person in the world. Her kindness and sweetness had meant so much to Gennie, who had come from an unhappy home, that she had given her heart to the young girl she tended. When she married, Gennie would gladly have gone with her to the North Pole, had she asked her to do so.

Although she had never said so, Gennie had always hated living in England with servants who did not understand who often laughed at her and teased her simply because she was different.

It had been an inexpressible relief when they had left the Big House.

At the same time, Gennie had never forgiven the Earl for his behaviour towards her beloved mistress.

If Theresa hated her father, no one had any idea that Gennie had for him a bitter loathing that would have made her murder him if she had had the opportunity.

It tore her in pieces in the morning when she saw her Mistress's lovely face with dark shadows under her eyes and knew she had cried all night.

But there was nothing she could do except devote herself to her service and look after Theresa.

At first, after Theresa had been born, the Earl had seemed to be content to stay with his wife and be the head of what was now a family.

Then he was off again attracted by some pretty face he found irresistible, finding the gaiety of London far more to his liking than the quietness of the country and his responsibilities there.

Only Gennie knew how every time he came back her mistress would pray that he would stay and that he would find her love for him sufficient.

But it always became blatantly obvious what was his real reason for returning, and once he had got what he wanted he was off again to pastures new.

There was only left the tears that were concealed and an agony of loss which even the greatest self-control could not suppress.

"He was cruel and wicked!" Gennie exclaimed to herself and called down upon him all the mediaeval curses that she had learnt when she was a child from the witches who were part of the story of the Vosges mountains where she had been born.

As the years went by Gennie had learned to hide her feelings and also to accept the inevitable.

Although she was desperately apprehensive now as to what the future might hold for Theresa, she was too wise to go on saying so.

The only consolation, she told herself, was that if things became too difficult she would personally find some of her mistress's Chaufour relations and beg them to help her.

The carriage in which they were seated was comfortable, and they were just thinking it was time for the train to start when the door opened and another passenger got in.

She was a very pretty young lady dressed exceedingly smartly. In fact, overwhelmingly so, with an expensive sable fur coat over her arm.

She carried a large jewel-case which she placed carefully down on the seat beside her.

She tipped the Porter but not very generously, so that he only said *'Merci'* instead of *'Merci beaucoup, Madame'*.

Then as the door shut again and the Guard blew the whistle they knew they were off again.

Theresa stared at the newcomer, uncomfortably aware that it was rude to do so. Then she saw to her surprise that peeping out from under her skirts was a small dog.

She realised that the reason why he was so close to his

mistress was that she was holding him on too tight a lead so that his head was jerked upwards.

Then as the train gathered speed she released him, and immediately he moved away from her to shake himself, then jump up onto another seat.

He was a small, very pretty English spaniel with a reddish-brown coat and large appealing liquid eyes.

He sat down on the seat and immediately began to turn round and round to scratch his hind legs until his mistress said sharply in French:

"Stop that! Stop it at once, you horrible dog! If you have fleas I will throw you out at the next station!"

She spoke so aggressively that Theresa bent forward and said:

"Excuse me, *Madame,* but may I look at your dog? I do not think it is fleas that are biting him, but something else."

"Whatever it is, he is not to scratch!" the newcomer said. "I do not like dogs anyway. They are a nuisance!"

Theresa was hardly listening.

She had moved to the other side of the carriage. After first patting the dog, then soothing him she felt his back legs and found that it was not in fact a flea that was troubling him but a burr.

She pulled it out and showed it to the young woman on the opposite seat.

"This is what was hurting him!"

"It looks horrible!" she said. "What is it?"

"It is a burr, a sharp clinging prickly seed, and comes from a plant which grows in the English fields."

"Then he is not likely to pick up another one."

"You are going to Paris?"

"I have an apartment, a very smart one, and I do not want a dog in it!"

"Then why have you brought him with you?" Theresa asked curiously.

"He was a present from a friend, a very *special* friend, and I could not refuse."

Theresa was stroking the dog with her hand and he was responding by cuddling close to her and nuzzling his nose against her.

"He is a very pretty little spaniel," she said. "What is his name?"

"It is very English," his mistress replied, "so of course I shall have to change it. It is *Rover*."

She pronounced it in such a funny way that Theresa laughed and said:

"That is very appropriate. Spaniels have a very roving nature, and they are also very good gun-dogs."

"That certainly does not interest me, and he will do no roving in Paris! But I dare say I can dispose of him."

Theresa hesitated a moment, then knowing she was being indiscreet she said:

"I will buy him from you, if you like."

Rover's mistress looked at her in astonishment.

"Buy him?" she exclaimed.

Then she gave a little laugh.

"That is certainly something I did not expect to hear!"

"I love dogs," Theresa explained, "and I think he would be happy with me."

She thought as she spoke that she was being very foolish.

At the same time, she could not bear the small English dog to suffer, which she was certain he would with the Frenchwoman who did not like dogs and certainly had no idea how to treat them.

As if she suddenly made up her mind, Rover's mistress said:

"He is yours! I give him to you! Do not thank me, because I am glad to be rid of him!"

"But I do thank you!" Theresa replied, "and I promise you I will look after him very well."

"I am not interested," the woman said. "I like people – not animals!"

"Now I think of it," Theresa replied, "I much prefer animals!"

The woman gave a laugh that was quite spontaneous.

"That is a very stupid remark, *Mademoiselle*, when you have a face like yours!"

Theresa looked at her in astonishment as she went on:

"Animals, especially dogs and cats, are messy, ugly and dirty!"

She laughed again before she continued:

"For you and me there is something far more interesting! Although they too are animals, they are called 'men'!"

Chapter Three

"I HATE men!"

The words came to Theresa's lips without her meaning to say them.

As she spoke she thought it was a mistake to be so familiar with a stranger.

Now the woman opposite was staring at her in astonishment.

"Hate men?" she repeated. "Then who is going to pay for your furs, your jewels, your beautiful gowns and all the other comforts of life?"

Now it was Theresa's turn to look astonished, and as she did so she realised that the woman sitting opposite must be one of the glamorous Courtesans about whom she had heard so much and for whom her father had extracted so much money from her mother.

She saw that the woman to whom she was talking was very heavily made up, far more so than might have been expected, even though it was fashionable now to wear powder and lip-salve.

She was also exceedingly smart.

Her hat was a mass of feathers and tilted at a provocative angle on her dark curly hair, her gown had the latest fashionable bustle which had replaced the crinoline.

Then Theresa noticed how much jewellery she was wearing.

There were diamonds glittering in her ears and round her neck beneath the collar of her velvet jacket. There were rings on her fingers and bracelets on her wrists and she was in fact, a picture of extravagance and *chic.*

As if she was amused by Theresa's scrutiny the woman said:

"Let us introduce ourselves. I am Celeste St. Clair and you will find when you reach Paris that my name is very well-known there."

She waited for Theresa to reply and after a moment she said hesitatingly:

"M . . my name is . . Theresa Beauvais."

"I am indeed delighted to meet you, *Mademoiselle,*" Celeste St. Clair replied, "but I cannot understand why you hate men! For I am not flattering you when I say that you are very pretty."

"Thank you," Theresa said. "I do not wish to speak about my feelings but merely to reach Paris and find somewhere where I can cook."

"Cook?" The word was almost a shriek from Celeste's painted lips. "But, why in the name of all the Saints, should you, looking as you do, wish to cook?"

Theresa chose her words with care.

"I have to earn my living," she said after a moment, "and as I am a very experienced Chef and have cooked for very important people, I hope there will be no difficulty in finding employment in a country which appreciates good food."

"That is true," Celeste agreed, "and even though *Milord* with whom I have been staying in England had a French Chef, the food was not what I would eat in Paris."

Theresa was silent for a moment. Then she said:

"Well, at least your friend had good taste when it comes to dogs!"

"His house is full of them," Celeste said disdainfully. "Too many dogs and not enough fires. I shall be glad to be back in Paris for that reason if for no other!"

She made it sound as though there were a great many other reasons. Then as if she wished to impress Theresa she said:

"Perhaps as you too have come from England you will have heard of my friend. He is Lord Ludgrove, and he has a very large house in Hertfordshire and a much more comfortable one in London."

Theresa shook her head.

"I have been living in the country and I am afraid I did not know many grand people."

"Then I hope you will enjoy yourself in Paris," Celeste said, "where I assure you there will be many men who will try to persuade you to do much more exciting things than cook their meals!"

She put a meaning into the words and there was an expression in her dark eyes which Theresa did not understand.

She was only trying to remember if she had ever heard of Lord Ludgrove, and wondering if she was right in thinking that Celeste St. Clair was one of the much-sought-after 'Ladies of Paris'.

It seemed strange that she should travel to England.

Almost as if she was reading her thoughts Celeste said:

"*Milord* was very rich, very generous, but old, and you must understand that while I am young and the whole of Paris admires me I waste myself in England."

Theresa laughed.

"I can understand that, and I am sure Paris is just as gay as I have always heard it is."

She thought as she spoke that what she had heard of the way her father had behaved in Paris with beautiful women who must have looked like Celeste revolted her.

When she remembered his behaviour towards her mother and how unkind he had been, she gave a little shrug and deliberately turned her eyes away from Celeste's sable coat and glittering jewels.

"I have been thinking," Celeste said after they had travelled for a little while in silence, "and I think I might be able to help you to find a position as a cook."

Instantly Theresa swept away her thoughts of her father and asked:

"Could you do that? It would be very kind, for to be truthful, I know nobody in Paris."

Celeste looked at her as if she was determined to know the truth as she asked:

"Did you really mean it when you said you hated men?"

"I hate them!" Theresa replied. "They are cruel, ruthless and selfish! I have sworn that I will never marry and never allow a man to hurt me as . . somebody I loved was . . hurt."

She faltered over the last words because she had been about to say: "my mother".

Theresa did not notice the strange expression in Celeste's face as if what she was thinking was somehow amusing and at the same time satisfying.

"I tell you what I will do, *Mademoiselle*," she said after a moment. "I will write to the secretary of the *Marquis* de Sare."

Theresa was listening intently as she went on:

"He is a very charming man and he looks after all the Marquis's houses and estates for him, in each one of which he has an experienced and what he considers a superlative Chef."

Theresa drew in her breath.

"And you think he might employ me?"

"You will not see him, at least not until you are established, but *Monsieur* Henri Brantome will engage you if he thinks you are good enough to please his master."

"That is very, very kind of you!" Theresa said, "and I do not know why you should be so generous to me."

"It is in return for taking Rover off my hands," Celeste replied. "I told *Milord* that I did not like dogs, but no

Englishman understands that. Like their horses they are far more important to them than women!"

She laughed even though there was a touch of bitterness in her voice and then said almost as if she spoke to herself:

"It is the same with all men. They have no respect, no real affection for anybody but themselves!"

Now there was undoubtedly a cynical note in her voice as she went on:

"The *Marquis* is exactly as you described men: cruel, ruthless and selfish. He thinks only of himself, and is quite unconcerned with anybody who is hurt by his behaviour!"

Theresa was listening wide-eyed and now she said:

"But you would send me to such a man?"

"Not *to* him," Celeste corrected scornfully, "but to cook for him, and I think if he ever discovers there is a woman in his kitchen, it will give him such a shock to know we have other interests besides amusing him."

There was a definite spitefulness in the way she spoke, and listening Theresa guessed that the *Marquis* de Sare had in some way hurt Celeste and she was now his enemy.

Celeste picked up her handbag and drew from it a little notecase. It was made of gold and had her initials picked out in diamonds in one corner.

She took out a card on which was printed her name and address, and scrawled on the back of it in a rather uneducated hand before she said:

"Give this to *Monsieur* Brantome. You will find him at Sare House in the Champs Élysèes. Anybody will tell you where it is."

Theresa took it from her and said:

"I am very, very grateful. I think it is exceedingly kind of you to help me in this way. Perhaps one day I shall be able to do you a service."

Celeste laughed.

"You have done that already, and you will find that Rover will make himself very much at home in one of the *Marquis*'s Châteaux, which I anticipate is where you will be sent."

Theresa's eyes went to the dog.

She had not dared to hope that she would find work in the country rather than Paris.

She had agreed with Gennie that it was the best thing to go to France, and obviously first to Paris, to find employment although because of her father, she had a horror of that City and everybody in it.

She was aware that it was unreasonable to feel like that, and yet she could not help it.

But she now thought that if only she with Gennie and Rover, could work somewhere in the country, it would not only be a far more pleasant arrangement but much more difficult, in fact almost impossible, for her Uncle to find her.

As if she had settled everything Celeste took off her elegant hat and with a yawn stretched herself out on the seat putting her head on her sable coat.

"I am tired," she said, "and is it surprising, when *Milord* found it very hard to let me go?"

She gave another yawn and because she was curious Theresa could not help asking:

"Does he love you?"

"Love? What is love?" Celeste asked. "He finds me entrancing and very different from the stuck-up young Englishwomen who look down their noses and get thick legs from all that walking!"

Theresa laughed.

"Is that how they appear to you?"

Celeste's eyes were closing and her eye-lashes heavy with mascara were very dark against her cheeks.

"What *Milord* said is true: Englishwoman are for breeding, Frenchwomen for pleasure!"

The last word was almost inaudible but Theresa heard it, and as she did so she realised that Gennie had heard it too.

Gennie, who was sitting at the other side of the carriage, beckoned her and she moved carefully to her side so as not to disturb Celeste.

As she sat down Gennie said in English:

"How can you talk to a woman like that, M'Lady? What your poor mother would say, I don't know!"

"She has been very kind," Theresa replied in a whisper, "and has given me an introduction where we might find employment with room for Rover."

The small dog had followed her as she moved and now he jumped up on the seat beside her and put his head on her lap.

He looked up at her with his large brown loving eyes as if he was beseeching her to be kind to him.

As she fondled him she said to Gennie:

"Everything is going to be all right, but do remember not to call me 'M'Lady'. We are just two ordinary Frenchwomen looking for work."

"Ordinary!"

Gennie muttered the word beneath her breath, and Theresa knew she was longing to protest further and denounce Celeste as an immodest and immoral woman.

She might be that, but Theresa could not help thinking there was something in what she had said about Englishwomen.

She had seen the Holme relations at her mother's Funeral and thought how excessively plain and ungainly they were. None of the women walked with any grace, and the black they had donned out of respect for the dead made their skins look sallow and appeared to accentuate all their bad points.

It made her sure that not only were her father's relatives censorious with regard to her mother because she was half-French, but also envious because she was so beautiful and, of course, rich.

"I will forget them, Mama!" she told herself.

But she could not help, however French she might pretend to be, having English thoughts and English feelings, and that meant that Celeste was an immoral and wicked woman with whom she should not associate.

Yet because they were together in a train that would take many hours to reach Paris, it was impossible not to respond to her friendliness, her frankness and what Theresa knew was an irresistible charm.

She was charming to the Porters who asked if there was anything they could get her from the stations at which they stopped; charming to the waiters who brought them food on trays to the carriage and were quite prepared to go back to fetch something they had forgotten to order, when Celeste requested it.

Each time they moved off again the Guard locked them in so that they should not be disturbed by other passengers.

It was the way Celeste spoke, the way she looked at them, and what Theresa knew was a warm femininity about her which appealed to them because they were men.

She tried to tell herself that she merely imagined it, but her mother had taught her to be perceptive, to use her instinct, and above all to look beneath the surface to discover somebody's true personality and character.

Celeste, she thought, might be an immoral woman, although she was not quite sure what that entailed, except that she knew that it was very wrong and wicked.

At the same time she was young, she enjoyed life, and she was very attractive.

By the time they reached Paris Theresa found herself thinking that in a way she could understand why her father had grown bored with the country and had preferred to spend time with women like Celeste. They must have made him laugh, and they had other allurements which she did not wish to think about.

Then she told herself she must be losing her wits, for there was no excuse for her father's behaviour, and she would hate him and despise him until her dying day.

******

When they reached the *Gare du Nord* Celeste, who had slept a great deal on the journey, exclaimed that she was exhausted and intended to go straight to bed and sleep for twenty-four hours.

"If you take my advice, *Mademoiselle*," she said, "you will do the same. It is no use trying to give an impression of great efficiency when you stumble over your words and cannot remember the answers to all the questions you will be asked.''

''I am sure you are right,'' Theresa said humbly, ''and as it is now very, very late, in fact nearly midnight, I wonder where my friend and I could find a respectable, quiet lodging-house?''

''I am sure there are hundreds such as you describe,'' Celeste said, ''but you would be safer in an *Hôtel.* I know of one in the Rue St. Honoré. It may be a little expensive for you, but at least you will not have to put up with any disagreeableness from the men you dislike so much!''

Theresa looked frightened.

It was something she had never anticipated, that there might be men who would perhaps talk to her and try to be friendly when she did not know them.

''Go to the *Hôtel du Louvre,*'' Celeste said, ''and I assure you the attention they give you there will make the expense worthwhile.''

''Thank you, I will take your advice, *Mademoiselle.*''

''As there will be somebody at the station to meet me,'' Celeste went on, ''we will say goodbye now.''

Theresa looked surprised and Celeste laughed before she added:

''You are far too pretty, *ma chère*, for me to take the risk of letting him see you!''

Now Theresa was astonished and thought Celeste must be joking.

Then as the train drew in at the platform she was leaning out of the window searching the platform until with a little cry of delight she was waving her expensively gloved hand.

As soon as the train came to a standstill and the door was opened she jumped out, and Theresa saw her throw her arms round a tall, good-looking man wearing a top-hat.

He was not very young, but his coat with a fur collar gave him an air of wealth that was unmistakable.

Then as two liveried servants who had obviously come with

him came into the carriage to collect Celeste's fur coat and her jewel-case she hurried him away up the platform without a backward glance at Theresa.

She and Gennie descended much more slowly and by the time they had collected their luggage of which there was a large pile, there was no sign anywhere of the delectable bejewelled lady with whom they had spent so many hours.

As they drove away from the station in a hired carriage towards the *Hôtel du Louvre* with Rover sitting on the seat beside them, Gennie said:

"I hope, M'Lady, you're going to tear up that woman's card! You don't want introductions of that sort!"

"Of course I want it!" Theresa said sharply. "Do not be so stupid, Gennie! We have nowhere else to go, and we do not even know where to enquire for the post for which we are looking."

"She's no good, and it's not on her introduction that you'll find yourself in any respectable household!" Gennie grumbled.

"As a Chef, whether I am a male or a female, I am not concerned with the behaviour of those who employ me," Theresa answered. "Besides, from the way she spoke I am sure that if we are in the country, we shall see very little of *Monsieur le Marquis*!"

"I hope you are right, M'Lady," Gennie said. "I keep thinking perhaps it would be better for you to do what your Uncle wishes and stay in England where you belong."

"I am not going to answer that," Theresa replied, "or I shall lose my temper. My uncle's plans for me are degrading and, as I told you, I have no intention of marrying anybody, least of all a member of the Holme family. They ignored me completely until they realised I was rich!"

Theresa did not argue further because she knew that Gennie was very tired.

In fact, by the time they reached the *Hôtel du Louvre* which was quiet and respectable, she was capable of doing very little more than yawning.

They were shown into two comfortable, if not luxurious

bedrooms and as soon as Theresa undressed she got into bed and fell asleep.

She was just aware before she did so that Rover had curled himself up on the foot of her bed and she felt as if he was there to protect her and look after her.

"If nothing else," she told him as she patted him goodnight, "I shall be very, very grateful to Celeste St. Clair for giving you to me."

******

It was late the next morning before she woke.

She rang for a page-boy to take Rover out for a walk, then dressed and enjoyed a breakfast of croissants and hot coffee, feeling full of the joys of Spring, and ready for any adventure that might come her way.

She thought it would be a mistake to take Rover with her to meet *Monsieur* Brantome and she was therefore obliged to leave him behind at the hotel while she drove in a carriage to the *Marquis* de Sare's house in the Champs Élysèes.

She expected it would be impressive and she did not miss the gold-tipped railings that surrounded it or the garden inside the very high iron gates.

Then she saw that the house itself seemed unusually large to be in a town.

The garden was a riot of spring flowers, the chestnut trees were just beginning to come into bud.

As the cab-driver got down to ring the bell for her with a politeness which Theresa felt was very French, she thought that if the *Marquis*'s house in the country in which she hoped to work was as beautiful as this, she would feel very much at home.

She asked the servant who came to the door if she could speak to *Monsieur* Brantome and was taken without any formality across a very finely decorated hall and along a wide passage hung with some magnificent pictures.

She was shown into what she realised was an office, and sitting at a desk she saw a man nearing middle-age who looked up with a worried expression on his face.

"A lady to see you, *Monsieur!*" the servant announced as Theresa walked in.

Monsieur Brantome rose to his feet.

Theresa thought he had a kind face and she held out Celeste's card to him saying:

"*Mademoiselle* Celeste St. Clair sent me to you, *Monsieur*, when I told her I was looking for employment as a Chef."

Monsieur Brantome took the card and stood without looking at it, staring at Theresa as if he had misunderstood what she had said.

Because she felt she should explain herself further Theresa said quickly:

"I met *Mademoiselle* St. Clair in the train yesterday on my way to Paris and when I told her I was looking for employment she sent me to you."

"As a Chef?"

There was no doubt of the astonishment in *Monsieur* Brantome's voice.

Theresa smiled.

"I assure you, *Monsieur*, I am a very good Chef, and I have references to prove it."

Because he seemed so bewildered by her appearance and had forgotten to invite her to sit down, Theresa seated herself in a hard chair which stood in front of the desk and, opening her handbag, took out the references she had written herself.

She handed them across the desk to *Monsieur* Brantome who sat down to read them.

He studied them carefully and she had the feeling that he was suspicious that they were not what they appeared to be, or else her appearance and her request was part of some joke.

He put the letters down in front of him on the desk and said:

"It seems incredible, *Mademoiselle*, if you will forgive my saying so, that anybody so young should aspire to being a Chef to a gentleman as fastidious and as knowledgeable about food as the *Marquis!*"

"I assure you, *Monsieur* Brantome," Theresa replied,

"that the two people for whom I have worked before, especially *Madame la Comtesse* Marie Chaufour, expected perfection at the table and were very complimentary about my efforts."

Unexpectedly *Monsieur* Brantome smiled, and it swept the worried look from his face.

"I think *Mademoiselle* St. Clair must be clairvoyant," he said, "or else she is aware that in the past good Chefs have been, even in France, difficult to find."

"I cannot believe that!"

"It is true!" *Monsieur* Brantome insisted. "And especially are they as rare as the Ibis bird when it means leaving Paris for the country."

Theresa clasped her hands together.

"*Mademoiselle* St. Clair suggested that perhaps *Monsieur le Marquis* would need a Chef in one of his Châteaux, and I would rather work in the country than anywhere else!"

"Can that be true?" *Monsieur* Brantome asked.

Theresa had the feeling that he almost added: "looking as you do."

"It is quite true," she insisted, "and I should tell you that I have with me an assistant, a Frenchwoman of some fifty years of age, who is very experienced in the culinary arts, and we also have a little dog, an English spaniel."

She thought as she spoke that if she were unable to take Rover with her she would have to look elsewhere. Already he seemed to have wound his way into her heart and in some ways made up for the ache in her breast ever since she had said goodbye to her horses at the Dower House.

She loved them passionately, but she knew that the grooms whom her mother had employed would look after them well. Even if her Uncle took them into his own stable they would be all right. He had many faults, but like all her Holme relatives he was a judge of horse-flesh and according to her father, an excellent rider.

"So you are fond of the country!" *Monsieur* Brantome was remarking.

"Very fond!" Theresa said firmly.

"In which case you might be happy, although I warn you it seems unlikely, in the Marquis's Château in the Basses-Pyrenees. I must be frank and tell you that one Chef after another has left because they could not bear what they called the boredom of the country, and having so little to do."

"You mean there is not much entertaining?"

"*Monsieur* very seldom goes there, except perhaps for two or three days at a time in the summer, but he expects the Château to be kept open all the winter in case he has a desire to visit it. But however well I pay the servants, only the old ones find it at all tolerable, while those who are younger leave after only a few months."

He paused before he added:

"I trust that you, *Mademoiselle*, are not in that category."

"I am not," Theresa replied. "I am very anxious to live in the country. I do not like towns, and I have no wish to be in Paris."

She could not help her voice sharpening as she thought of how her mother had hated the thought of Paris and all it entailed.

Then she thought that *Monsieur* Brantome looked at her curiously and she said quickly:

"Please, *Monsieur*, I promise that if you send me to the country, I will not let you down or come back complaining after a few months or even a year. The quieter my surroundings the better I shall be pleased."

She thought the Frenchman gave her a sharp look as if he suspected her motive for wishing to be hidden away.

Then he glanced down again at the references in front of him before he picked them up and handed them back to Theresa.

"When could you be ready to leave, *Mademoiselle* Beauvais?"

"As soon as you wish, *Monsieur*," Theresa replied. "My assistant and I arrived in Paris only last night and we are staying at the *Hôtel du Louvre* which is rather expensive, so it would be best for us to get down to work as soon as possible."

She hoped as she spoke that what she said sounded plausible, and *Monsieur* Brantome picked up his pen and said:

"I know your name, *Mademoiselle*, so perhaps you would also give me the name of your assistant."

He wrote it down on the pad in front of him and said:

"I think you will find that the old servants at the Château will do their best to make you comfortable, but because I am very anxious for you, *Mademoiselle*, to settle there, I hope you will ask me if there is anything special I can do for you."

Theresa already had an answer to this.

"I would like, *Monsieur*, separate bedrooms for myself and my assistant, and if it is possible, a small Sitting-Room where we can be alone."

She knew it was not only because she had no wish to sit with the other staff, but that Gennie would think she was degrading herself by associating too closely with servants who should be waiting on her, as befitted her position by birth.

"And what is my position now?" Theresa asked herself a little bitterly. "I am a refugee from my own country! A fugitive from my Guardian and from all other men besides!"

She could almost see herself streaking like a fox across-country with the fox-hounds after her in full cry.

Then she listened as *Monsieur* Brantome said:

"The Château is a very large one, and what you are asking, *Mademoiselle*, presents no problems. I will send a note saying what you require to the *Maître d'Hôtel* who is in charge when I am not there, and as I suspect you do not know France I will send a Courier with you on the journey who will also make sure of your comfort once you arrive."

"That is very good of you, *Monsieur*."

She rose to her feet and *Monsieur* Brantome said with a smile:

"You are not very practical, *Mademoiselle!* You have not yet asked me what your wages will be."

"No, of course not!" Theresa said quickly. "I forgot!"

"That is not usual where French Chefs are concerned," he

remarked, "but I must of course enquire what you are asking for your services."

Theresa tried to think what her mother had paid the Chef in the old days in the Big House, but could not remember.

"As I am new to Paris, and have been away from my own country for sometime, I think I should leave it to you, *Monsieur*, to be fair and just and give me what you think I am worth."

Monsieur Brantome laughed.

"That is certainly surprising, *Mademoiselle*, but as you say, I will be 'fair and just'. If you give satisfaction, there will be no difficulty about adjusting your salary later to a higher figure."

He then said he would pay Theresa what seemed to her quite a large sum of money, and half that amount for Gennie.

She accepted quickly, thinking that things had gone so well and it was thanks entirely to Celeste St. Clair that there need be no worries about the immediate future.

Only when she rose to say goodbye did *Monsieur* say hesitatingly, as if he was feeling for words:

"I hope you will not think it impertinent, *Mademoiselle*, but as you are so young, and although you tell me you are experienced, you certainly do not look it. I suggest that you do not become involved with any of the guests who stay at the Château from time to time."

The way he spoke made Theresa quite certain that he meant men.

She stiffened before she said in a hard voice which was very different from the way she had been speaking before:

"You may rest assured, *Monsieur*, I have no wish to be involved with anybody, and I shall keep my place, which is in the kitchen!"

She did not wait to see what she was sure would be an expression of surprise in *Monsieur* Brantome's eyes, but walked resolutely across the room towards the door.

He hurried to open it for her and they walked side by side down the passage.

As they reached the hall he asked:

"What was the weather like in England when you were there?"

"Dull, overcast and rather cold," Theresa replied.

As she spoke she had a glimpse through an open door of sunshine and flowers.

"Then I am sure France will be a very welcome contrast," *Monsieur* Brantome said, and added: "I hope, *Mademoiselle*, you will be very happy at the Château. The train leaves at ten o'clock and I will instruct the Courier to collect you tomorrow morning at the *Hôtel du Louvre* an hour earlier. He will of course buy your tickets for you and see that you are provided with every comfort on the journey."

"Thank you, *Monsieur*, thank you very much!"

Theresa shook hands with him then stepped into the carriage which on her instructions when she had left the *Hôtel* was open.

As she drove away she waved to *Monsieur* Brantome and lay back.

As the horse moved down the Champs Élysèes she wanted to cry aloud her delight that she had succeeded in getting exactly what she wanted: not only a place to go, but a place that was in the country.

"I am lucky, so very lucky!" she told herself and said the same words when she told Gennie what had occurred.

As they had the rest of the day to themselves they wandered round the streets looking in the shop windows and ate *pâtisseries* on the pavement outside a café.

"I can make them better than this!" Theresa remarked.

"I should hope so!" Gennie replied, but Theresa knew that actually she was enjoying them.

They were not tired when they returned to the *Hôtel* and Theresa said:

"Why do we not go out tonight and dine at a Restaurant? I know it would not be correct if we were in England, but after all who is to know in Paris?"

"We'll do nothing of the sort, M'Lady!" Gennie said sharply. "We'll have dinner at the *Hôtel* and not do anything so foolish as to go looking for trouble, which is what you'd be doing."

"What sort of trouble?" Theresa asked.

"Men!" Gennie said. "Didn't you see how those Frenchmen were eyeing you outside the cafè?"

"No, I never saw them!" Theresa replied.

Gennie bit back the words that were on her lips.

She had been aware as she had never been before, how Theresa's beauty had caught the eye of every man in the vicinity.

She was not, the old maid thought, as beautiful as her mother had been, and yet there was a freshness and something different about her which seemed to vibrate almost like sunshine.

Even the waiters who served them smiled at her in admiration and kept coming back to the table to ask if there was something more she wanted.

"The sooner we get to the country the better!" Gennie said sharply. "We'll eat here tonight, M'Lady, and no nonsense about it!"

She left Theresa and went into her own bedroom shutting the door sharply behind her.

Theresa sat down on the bed.

"It is sad, Rover," she said to the little dog who was nuzzling up to her, "but we are not able to do anything exciting until we are too old to enjoy it."

Theresa held him close to her and hugged him as she said:

"But we will enjoy the country, you and I. We can go for long walks, you will be able to chase rabbits, and there will be nobody to upset us or try to make us do anything we do not want to do."

She wondered how long it would be before her Uncle realised that she had left her home and was not coming back.

She reckoned that it would be a week or ten days before he moved into the Big House, and then he might begin to make enquiries as to her whereabouts.

She was relieved to know that with the wages she would receive for cooking for the Marquis there would be no need to dip into what she thought of as her 'nest-egg' – the money she and Gennie had hidden on them.

She played with the idea of putting it into a Bank in Paris, then decided it would be far better if she banked it in the nearest town to the Château, so that it would be available if ever she wanted it suddenly.

It struck her that 'suddenly' might mean that something had happened at the Château that she did not like.

She could not help thinking of the way in which *Monsieur* Brantome had warned her not to get involved with any of the guests.

Then as she began to think about it, she realised that the *Marquis* must be unmarried. This was unusual for a French nobleman because she knew their marriages were arranged when they were very young.

Moreover, if he was involved with somebody like Celeste St. Clair, then he would behave in the same way as her father had done.

She felt a little shudder of fear pass through her as she told herself she must be very, very careful to keep out of his way.

And she would be even more careful to have enough ready money to leave the Château at any moment she wished to do so.

'Perhaps until we are quite certain there are no pitfalls,' she thought, 'it would be wiser to keep the money with us.'

Later that evening just before they were going down to dinner Gennie came into her bedroom to say:

"I want to talk to you, M'Lady."

Theresa who had just had a bath, was arranging her hair in front of the mirror.

She looked round with a smile to say:

"What is it now? And do stop calling me 'M'Lady'!"

"That's how I am thinking of you at the moment," Gennie said firmly, "and I have decided it would be a mistake for us to go the Château tomorrow."

Theresa turned round again from the mirror to stare at her.

"A mistake? Why?"

There was a moment's pause and she knew that Gennie was feeling for words before she replied:

"I've been talking downstairs to some of the staff, and they've been telling me about the *Marquis* de Sare."

"I can guess what they said about him," Theresa said, "and I am not going to listen!"

Gennie came closer to her and said:

"You have to listen to me, M'Lady. It's not right or proper for you to be under the same roof as a man who's notorious for his love-affairs and who's at one time been the Protector of that painted woman we met in the train!"

"I guessed that," Theresa said, "and he must have let her down, because she was so very bitter about him."

"You guessed?" Gennie exclaimed, her voice rising. "What would your mother have thought about you having ideas like that?"

She made a sound that was almost a sob before she said:

"Oh, M'Lady, let's go back to England! It is not right for you to be associating with the dregs of the gutter, and with the *Marquis* of Sare."

"I am not going to *associate* with him," Theresa said quietly, "I am going to *cook* for him. I will not see him eat what I have prepared, and I doubt if I will even come in contact with him."

She saw that Gennie was going to argue and said crossly:

"Oh, Gennie, do not be so stupid! Did you ever know Papa to look at one of the maids when he lived at the Big House, or do anything when he was at home that was in the least reprehensible?"

She thought for a moment, then went on:

"I remember him saying once when someone we knew ran away with a Governess, that no decent man fouled his own nest."

Gennie drew in her breath.

"That's all very well, M'Lady, but your father was an Englishman, and however badly he behaved to your mother, we were not supposed to know about it. But you'll be under the same roof as the Marquis."

"If the Château is as large as the Big House we might just as well be in another country!" Theresa replied. "I remember how you used to grumble because it was such a long way from the kitchens to Mama's bedroom, and the Sewing-Room was up two floors!"

She saw that Gennie was slightly appeased and went on:

"I was just thinking before you came in that if anything goes wrong, if the Marquis in any way frightens us, we have plenty of money and I am not going to put it into a Bank until I am quite sure we have settled down and want to stay."

She finished arranging her hair and added:

"If we get nervous, Gennie dear, we can just jump into a train and go somewhere else, perhaps to Italy. I have always wanted to see Rome."

Gennie gave a little laugh.

"Oh, M'Lady, I don't know what to say to you, I really don't! I'm only trying to think what's best, and look after you. But I'm afraid, terribly afraid that you've 'jumped from the frying-pan into the fire' and will find yourself in real trouble!"

"If I am," Theresa said lightly, "I am quite certain you will rescue me."

She rose as she spoke and walked to the window.

It had a view over the roofs of Paris and behind them the sun was sinking in a blaze of glory.

"This is an adventure, Gennie," she said quietly. "I am free, and nobody is going to force me to do anything I do not want to do. I know in my heart that Mama is looking after me, and with her and you beside me how can I come to any harm?"

There was silence after she had spoken and she turned round to see tears running down the old maid's cheeks.

She put her arms around her saying:

"It is all right, Gennie. I promise you it will be all right! And at least you and I will be together, with Rover!"

Chapter Four

LE MARQUIS de Sare took a sip from his glass of wine and knew suddenly that he was bored.

He was attending one of the most exotically extravagant parties he had ever known and yet at the end of it he felt the whole evening was indigestible like a surfeit of pâté de foie gras.

It had been given for one of the most famous of *'Les Grandes Horizontales'* by a nobleman who was wooing the present mistress of the Prince Napoleon. It had surpassed in extravagance and inventiveness every orgy that had ever preceded it.

The dinner had included dishes that had come from all parts of the world, and were each as unique as the peacock tongues which had whetted the appetite of the Romans.

It had been followed by *Les Tableaux Plastiques* which made the *Kama Sutra* look like a religious tract, and the dance-floor had been strewn with the most expensive orchids that Paris could provide.

There had been also, the Marquis recalled, unusual little touches, like the five-thousand-franc note which rested under the passion-fruit sorbet presented to each lady.

There were also diamond charms which were drawn from a golden vase for those whose number at the table corresponded with that attached to each charm.

There were superlative wines which of course, like *Les Tableaux Plastiques*, had inflamed the senses of the guests, and looking round the room where the lights had been discreetly shaded, the *Marquis* saw that practically every guest except himself was indulging in intimacies which in his opinion should only take place behind closed doors.

He was well aware that his partner at the table, who was also his current mistress, was enticing him with every wile in her repertoire to enjoy himself in the same way.

As it happened, he was familiar with all of them and he was still behaving with dignity and self-control which was characteristic of him.

In fact, as he looked critically at what was going on, the cynical lines running from his nose to his mouth deepened and there was a contemptuous expression in his eyes which was unmistakable.

"Chéri," Jeanne was saying as she touched him with her long thin fingers and lifted her very attractive face to his, pouting her lips provocatively.

As the *Marquis* looked at her he caught sight of the edge of the five-thousand-franc note which, like most of the other women present, she had tucked down the front of her bodice. It was now partially hiding the exquisite curve of one of her tip-tilted breasts.

For some unknown reason, this offended something ultra-fastidious within him, a feeling which had a habit of occurring inconveniently and when he least expected it.

The *Marquis* was suddenly aware that not only was he bored with the voluptuousness of the party, but he had also finished with his present mistress.

He knew that tomorrow he would tell Brantome to send her a very generous cheque, and ask her to move as soon as possible from the house in which he had installed her on the edge of the Bois.

The house had had a succession of occupants over the years. The *Marquis* had found it a convenient place in which to keep his mistresses, first because he could visit it without anybody being aware that he was doing so, and secondly because he had arranged that it contained every possible comfort that he found essential in his own life.

Excellent servants, a cellar where he could keep his wines at the correct temperature, a bathroom, and a view from the windows which he enjoyed.

Naturally there was also his own linen, his own silver and most important of all, as it happened, his own pictures.

The *Marquis* had made it a rule never to entertain his mistresses except in the Reception Rooms of his house in the Champs Élysees.

When he gave parties like the one in which he was participating at the moment, they were never in what he thought of as his 'Family House'.

The reason for this was it jarred on him to think that his ancestors should look down disapprovingly on anything he did and dare to criticise him.

Abruptly he rose to his feet.

"You are not leaving, Fabian?" Jeanne asked with a little scream.

"It is growing late," the *Marquis* replied, "and I am tired."

"Non! Non! Mon cher, let us stay a little longer. It is so amusing, and I am sure there are more entertainments that we have not yet seen!"

The *Marquis* thought that nothing could possibly exceed in eroticism anything which had already taken place. But he did not say so and merely walked towards the door.

Still protesting, stumbling a little over her elaborate, over-decorated gown, his mistress followed him, and nobody took any notice of them as they left the room.

Only when they were outside in the hall did Jeanne say plaintively:

"I cannot think why you must leave the best and most expensive party that has ever been given in Paris!"

"An over-expensive, indecent orgy, in the worst possible taste!" the *Marquis* remarked.

He spoke sharply, and as if she realised it would be a mistake to argue with him, Jeanne slipped her hand through his arm and said:

"Then we will go home, *Mon cher*, and that after all will be much more amusing for us."

The *Marquis* knew as she spoke that she was somewhat piqued that he had not made any effort to embrace her, or even put his arm around her as every other gentleman was doing to his partner, and a great deal more besides.

Although she had been his mistress for some months Jeanne still had no idea of the *Marquis*'s violent dislike of exhibitionism, especially where it concerned himself.

As they reached the front door servants hurried to put the *Marquis*'s red-lined evening-cape over his shoulders and to hand him his tall hat, his gloves and his cane, while other flunkeys found the ermine-trimmed cape which matched Jeanne's gown.

He stood still while they did so, and not until a Linkman outside announced: "The carriage for *Monsieur le Marquis de Sare!"* did he start to walk towards the door.

Jeanne following him staggered for a moment and was in danger of losing her balance.

As the *Marquis*'s rather hard lips tightened in a thin line he was all the more certain that he had no wish to have any more contact with Jeanne Tourbey, lovely though she was.

Her lover before the *Marquis* had been the *Duc* de Morny.

It had been a challenge to take her from the *Duc* who had been jealous and extremely angry at losing her.

But like so many of his conquests the *Marquis* had found that what had glittered so tantalisingly in the distance was at close-quarters nothing but tinsel.

He helped Jeanne into the carriage and as the horses moved off she flung herself against him.

"Now at last we are alone, *chéri*."

She was being over-theatrical and, as the *Marquis* knew, slightly worried because he had obviously not enjoyed himself and afraid, in some way, she was not intelligent enough to analyse, that it was her own fault.

She was not yet aware that their liaison was at an end, and the *Marquis* knew that if he were to say so now, there would be tears, hysterics, pleadings and recriminations, all of which was something he had every intention of avoiding.

When other men dispensed with their mistresses, whether they were of the *Monde* or the *demi-Monde*, they did so without trouble and with the minimum amount of argument.

For him it was different, and he knew without conceit that it was not only because the women on whom he bestowed his favour were losing his money, but because despite themselves, they had given him their hearts.

It was understood, especially in France, that when a professional *experte de sciences galantes* came under a gentleman's protection, he rewarded her generously and she was faithful, attentive and prepared to do everything asked of her.

Then when the gentleman brought the arrangement to an end, she accepted it in a business-like manner, only making sure she received a satisfactory pay-off for the pleasure she had given.

But where the *Marquis* was concerned, there was nothing business-like about it.

He knew as they drove towards the house near the Bois that when Jeanne learned tomorrow what he intended, she would undoubtedly make a scene which would reverberate through the whole of Paris.

One of *La Garde,* and there were twelve of them who were the acknowledged Queens of their Profession, she could pick and choose her lovers, and thinking back, the *Marquis* was aware that she had been only too willing to leave the *Duc* de Morny, once she realised that he wanted her.

Because the *Marquis* was so domineering and insisted upon having his own way, Jeanne had even agreed to leave her own home.

The *Duc* de Morny had furnished the house she owned and she was exceedingly fond of it. Nobody except the *Marquis* could have persuaded her to live elsewhere.

Each of *La Garde* vied with one another in the extravagance of their furnishings, the comfort of their Salons and the amazing fixtures in their bathrooms.

In the *Hôtel* of La Priva the bath was solid onyx and the three gilt taps were set with precious stones.

The locks on the doors were said to be worth 2,000 francs apiece, and the staircase was made – steps, baluster and all – entirely of onyx.

Jeanne Tourbey had not yet aspired to such heights.

But if the *Marquis* moved her from her own background, to his then she had reasoned he must certainly pay for it, and she had already ordered designs for a staircase in crystal, gold and ebony.

But before a house could be considered, as every member of her profession knew, the first step was jewels!

Oscar Massin, one of the most famous Jewellers in Paris, catered not only for the Empress but for the most successful of *Les Grandes Horizontales* offering them jewelled flowers, ears of corn, sprays of eglantine, and lilies-of-the-valley.

He vied with Lemonnier and Fontenay, whose enormous necklaces, bracelets and ear-rings were worn with the same flourish with which a soldier carried home a flag captured on the battle-field.

The *Marquis* was exceedingly generous when it pleased him, had already given Jeanne a necklace and ear-rings of sapphires and diamonds which had made her contemporaries extremely envious.

She told herself now before the carriage came to collect her that she had already worn them four times in public, and tomorrow she would persuade him to visit Fontenay for a set in a different stone.

As they drove towards the Bois she whispered in his ear suggestions that occurred to her after she had watched the *Tableaux Plastiques.*

The horses came to a stand-still and the *Marquis* stepped

out to assist Jeanne to alight and took her up the steps to the front door which had already been opened by the night footman.

As Jeanne went ahead of him into the attractive hall he said:

"Goodnight, my dear!"

She stopped, then turned to stare at him, her eyes wide with surprise.

"You are not staying?"

"I am tired and tomorrow I am leaving early for the country."

"Leaving for the country?"

She found it hard to repeat the words.

Then because her senses were somewhat bemused by the quantity of wine she had imbibed, she had not even begun to protest before the *Marquis* with a perfunctory bow over her hand had turned to leave.

Before however, he could reach the door, with a shrill cry she had flung herself at him, and her arms were round his neck.

He tried to fend her off but her lips were seeking his and at the same time she was murmuring endearments.

She was trying to entice him with words, and with the exotic movements of her body against his.

Firmly the *Marquis* removed her arms from his neck.

"I am tired."

The words were sharp, his voice cold and determined.

Jeanne hesitated and was lost. The *Marquis* freed himself, had walked down the stairs and was inside his carriage before she could think of another way to prevent him leaving.

"Fabian! Fabian!" she cried out, but it was too late. The carriage door was shut and the horses were moving off.

She could only stand watching him go, feeling, although she hoped she was being imaginative, that he was leaving and she would not see him again.

The *Marquis* meanwhile sat back and putting his feet up on the opposite seat began to plan where he would go.

He told himself that the only way to avoid what he knew

would be a great deal of unpleasantness would be to leave Paris.

He was used to women telling him that they loved him in a way they had never loved anybody before.

'Love' was not a word he ever wished to associate with his mistresses but it was something they unfortunately could not avoid.

He liked women, he found them fascinating, alluring, but in one aspect, and one aspect only.

Companionship and intellectual interests, which in his case were very considerable, were something he shared only with his men-friends, and did not expect more of a woman than that she should be beautiful and please him sexually.

Apart from that, they were no more a part of his life than were his horses which could be returned to the stables when he was not using them.

He had learned when he was very young not to expect more than a woman, or a man, was capable of giving.

He did not consciously think of himself as being unique and yet he knew he was different from a great number of his friends and contemporaries.

Those who became obsessed with women seldom had many other interests in their lives, and the majority had none.

The *Marquis* however was concerned with very many different activities of which the majority of the people with whom he associated in the Social World, knew nothing.

He had no wish for the public to be aware that he was interested in politics, but often Statesmen and Politicians consulted him privately.

He was perhaps the one man in Paris at this moment who was aware that France was on a collision course to destruction from which he could see no way of saving her.

He was personally very disturbed, although nobody would listen to him, by the secret reports he obtained by his own methods of the build-up of arms and men in Prussia.

But he still tried because he believed it his duty to make the Minister of Defence, the *Duc* de Graumont, aware of what was happening.

Because he had, as he might have expressed it himself, so many fingers in so many pies, it suited him to be thought of as a frivolous partaker of the joys of Paris.

This meant that he was seen continually with beautiful women, and naturally the most outstanding of *'La Garde'*.

Of course, as he was aware, this had its dangers, and he knew that every wise General was alert to the moment when it was best to retire and live to fight another day.

"I will go to the country," the *Marquis* told himself as his horses drew him down the Champs Élyèes and in through the gold-tipped gates. "The question is – where?"

Then almost as if it was an inspiration, he remembered he had not visited his Château in the Basses Pyrennes for a very long time.

The reason for this was that it was a long way from Paris and he had had very many calls on his time in the City. And yet he had always thought of the Château as home because he had lived there as a small boy.

Now, as if he needed the comfort and security of it like a safe harbour from a turbulent sea, he knew where to go.

He walked into the hall and, although it was now two o'clock in the morning, he had the idea that it was just possible that Brantome was still up. This was not only because his secretary had an enormous amount of work to get through and was so conscientious that he invariably kept late hours. It was also because Henri Brantome was a bad sleeper. He had often said to the *Marquis* when he remonstrated with him:

"I would rather work at my desk, *Monsieur*, than lie awake doing it in my mind."

The *Marquis* had laughed, but he had understood and now as he half-expected when he opened the door of the Office he found his secretary sitting at his desk.

There was a pile of letters beside him he had obviously just written and Brantome looked up at the *Marquis* in surprise before rising to his feet.

"You are home, *Monsieur?"* he asked unnecessarily.

"I had an idea I would find you working," the *Marquis*

said, "and it makes it easier for me to tell you my plans now rather than leave a message with the servants."

"Your plans?"

"I am leaving for Château Sare tomorrow. Have my private carriage connected with the fastest train available. There is no reason for you to come with me. I am not going to give any parties or have any guests to stay. I just wish for a rest."

"For a rest?" his secretary questioned. "That is something I have never known you take for years!"

The *Marquis* laughed.

"I suppose that is true, but if I am bored I will send you a list of people I would like to invite, and you can arrange for them to join me as quickly as possible."

"You are really going alone, *Monsieur?*"

His question made the *Marquis* remember Jeanne whom he had for the moment forgotten.

"That reminds me," he said. "Give *Mademoiselle* Jeanne Tourbey the usual cheque, and ask her to move into her own house as soon as it is convenient."

For a moment Henri Brantome forgot that he should not, in any circumstances appear surprised at anything the *Marquis* said or did, and without meaning to, he exclaimed:

"You have finished with her?"

"Yes, finished!" the *Marquis* said and for once did not seem to mind that the question was an intrusion on his privacy.

"What is more, if you are interested, Brantome, I found the party this evening both overdone and boring. It will undoubtedly be the talk of Paris, but then as you know, Paris has nothing better to do but talk!"

There was a bitterness in his voice which Brantome did not miss.

"Was your meeting with the *Duc* at all helpful?" he asked.

The *Marquis* shook his head.

'He agrees with all I said with regard to the intentions of the Prussians. At the same time, he is convinced in his own mind that the French Army is as up-to-date and as well-prepared as the Generals tell him it is!"

"But he must have read your report?"

"He *says* he has read it," the *Marquis* answered, "but he listens to the Empress, who is determined that France shall show all Europe how strong, patriotic and magnificent she is!"

There was silence as the *Marquis* stopped speaking.

"But you will go on trying to convince the *Duc* of the truth?"

"I shall go on trying, Brantome," he answered, "but God knows if the *Duc* will listen to me!"

He went from the Office as he spoke.

Only as his secretary heard his footsteps dwindling away into the distance did he sit down again to think despairingly that the French as a nation were destroying themselves in their pursuit of pleasure.

One day they would wake up to reality and find it was too late.

The *Marquis* was thinking very much the same thing as his valet helped him undress in silence, then he got into bed.

He put out the light to lie in the dark in the comfortable magnificence of the four-poster bed which had been in his family for generations and in which he himself had been born.

But he did not give one thought to what had happened earlier in the evening.

He had always had the power to dismiss completely from his mind anything he disliked or disapproved of or which no longer interested him.

It was not only the party that had vanished from his thoughts but also the woman who had excited him until he had won her, then proved, as so many of her sex had done before, to be a disappointment.

If he had thought of Jeanne, he might have asked, as he had asked himself on numerous other occasions in the same circumstances, what he was looking for.

He was not certain what it was, but he was sure that it was unobtainable – a note of music that one sensed but could not quite hear.

It was like a distant horizon which one knows is there but is too far away for the eye to see.

Or perhaps a subtle perfume that is so elusive that one cannot describe it to one's self.

******

The *Marquis* had had a very strange life.

He had been married when he was quite young by the arrangement of his parents, to the daughter of Prince Louis de Bondy, which was in every way a suitable alliance.

The *Marquis* was rich, had great possessions, and also an honoured title which had been prominent frequently in the history of France.

The Princess was related to many of the reigning Monarchs in Europe, but was not particularly well-endowed with worldly goods.

It was an arrangement which gave immense satisfaction to the parents of the bride and bridegroom.

Unfortunately the moment the young couple found themselves as man and wife they took an instant and overwhelming dislike to each other.

Nevertheless, the *Marquis* who from the cradle had evinced a strong personality, told himself he must do his duty and produce an heir which was essential for the continuance of the Sare family.

But he had found it almost impossible to make himself even touch the Princess, let alone kiss her.

She, for her part, informed him at the first opportunity that she disliked him intensely and was already in love with one of her father's secretaries.

They spent their honeymoon quarrelling fiercely with each other, occupying separate bedrooms, and on returning to the *Marquis*'s house in Paris both were determined to see as little of each other as possible.

This was not difficult in a City which offered the *Marquis* every possible gaiety that any man could desire, and the Princess had the joy of having unlimited money to spend on jewels and clothes.

She was not exactly plain, but she certainly had not the allure or beauty of the women who found the *Marquis* irresistible, and who welcomed him into their midst with outstretched arms.

His reputation was sealed by the way he behaved then, enjoying himself like a small boy who had suddenly been let loose in a sweet-shop.

Before his marriage he had at home been very much under his father's thumb, and he had been perfectly content riding horses, racing, boar-hunting, and finding innumerable other country pursuits to fill his days.

He had also spent nearly two years going round the world, which his father had considered good for his education.

He himself had found it a fascinating experience which enriched his mind and strengthened his character in a way his family had not expected.

He had on his return agreed to the arranged marriage because he accepted it was traditional and there seemed on the surface no good reason why he should object to what from a social point of view was both brilliant and desirable.

But he had been so busy learning to play the part of a French aristocrat that for the moment he had forgotten he was also a man.

His proximity to the Princess made him vitally aware of that, with the result that disappointed in his marriage he inevitably sought a new interest.

This was women, a subject which he had not before explored.

He might have got into serious trouble where his family was concerned if two things had not occurred.

First his father died unexpectedly, which meant that he was now the *Marquis* de Sare.

Then fortunately, for him, although from her family's

point of view it was a tragedy, his wife was killed in a carriage accident.

It was something which happened fairly frequently in the over-crowded twisting streets of Paris which the Emperor was intending to have replanned by Baron Haussman.

The Princess's death contributed to the evidence that reform was urgently needed, and by the end of the same year Baron Haussman's plans for a new Paris were accepted.

The ancient, filthy houses with their insanitary foundations, the twisting, stinking streets which were a danger both to vehicles and pedestrians alike, were demolished.

For the *Marquis* to be free from his unhappy marriage at the age of twenty-two and to be his own master now that he was head of the family, was an exciting experience.

As a widower he could enjoy himself with women without a prickle of conscience or the disapproval of his relatives.

He took full advantage of the situation by first of all avoiding what should have been a long and hypocritical period of mourning by travelling to Africa, Egypt and Turkey which he had not visited before.

On his return he began to live in a state to which his father had never aspired, and to increase his already large fortune by his very intelligent handling of his finances which astonished those who thought they were his financial advisers.

He found it almost too easy to make money if one was clever, and therefore became involved in Politics because it was more difficult, and certainly less predictable.

But even the most busy man was entitled to his hours of relaxation, and as the Second Empire was a Paradise of beautiful women, they flocked to the *Marquis* like bees to a honey-pot.

It was considered essential for all gentlemen of means to vie with one another in having not only the most beautiful mistress obtainable, but also in decking her out in jewels so that she could outshine her rivals in *la vie de joie*.

The Emperor, although he had married for love, did not conceal his desire for other women and one of his first mistresses was 'La Castaglione', a beautiful woman without much brain.

If the Emperor made no secret of his love-affairs, what could High Society do but follow him?

The Prinçe Napoleon flaunted his mistresses, Baron Haussman when not actually engaged on his plans for a new Paris was seen unashamedly driving in his carriage with the beautiful young actress Francine.

The King of the Netherlands who spent more time in Paris than in his own country, was infatuated with *Madame* Musard.

Her parties, rather like the one the *Marquis* had just attended and which had bored him, were always exotic and extremely expensive.

The *Marquis* did not over indulge himself for long.

In fact, he found himself, as he became more and more discerning, growing more quickly dissatisfied and inevitably more fastidious.

When he chose a woman as his recognised mistress, she had to be as rare and as different as a new species of orchid or one of the perfect pearls which Oscar Massin showed him proudly as soon as he had acquired it.

Even so, when the first pride of possession was past, he would send the woman away.

He knew that in this he was different from other men.

Just as he had learned when he married that it was impossible for him to make love to his wife so he found that the moment his mistresses failed him – for that was how he thought of it – he could no longer, even out of kindness, show them any form of attention.

The curtain had come down, the play was ended, and there would never be another performance.

"How can you be so ruthless?" one of the *Marquis*'s friends once asked him. "I am not in the least in love as I once was with Ninon but because she adores me I have not the heart to dispense with her completely!"

"I see no point in prolonging the agony of what is the inevitable end of an *affaire de coeur*," the *Marquis* had replied coldly.

His friend had laughed.

"The trouble with you, Fabian, is that you are never concerned with your heart. Your body, yes, and perhaps your mind, but never, never with the organ that beats so passionately in all of us."

"Nonsense!" the *Marquis* said sharply.

At the same time he admitted to himself that his friend might have been speaking the truth.

Now, as if the thought of women was no longer interesting, he told himself with a feeling of satisfaction that Brantome would clear up the mess.

In the morning he would be on his way out of Paris and out of reach of Jeanne's clinging arms.

He would go to Château Sare and enjoy himself there as he always did and do what he had not done for sometime, which was to think.

It was really a case of mental stock-taking, and he also felt on those occasions when he was away either at sea or in the country that he drew into himself fresh power.

It was something magnetic, something vivid and alive which was very necessary to him.

He could not explain it except that he was strongly aware that it was part of his make-up.

He had first discovered it when as a youth he had visited the small State of Nepal which lies in the foothills of the Himalayas.

It was then that he had looked up at the snow-covered shining peaks above him and had known that, figuratively speaking, he must climb to the top of them.

Only when he had done so would he fulfil himself.

After that, at various times in his life when he had to make crucial decisions, or when events made them for him, he had always been aware that he could see mentally the picture, as if it was engraved on his soul, of the Himalayas brilliant in the sunshine.

He would know then that whatever he desired, whatever the goal, however difficult, he could achieve it.

He did not always think consciously of them, and yet they

were there: the glittering mountain peaks, and the vast foothills between himself and the shining glory of them.

******

In his comfortable railway-coach which he had designed himself and where he was waited on by two servants, the *Marquis* closed his eyes so as not to watch the countryside speeding past the window.

But he was not asleep, he was thinking.

He felt as if his thoughts roamed far away from Paris all over the world.

For the first time in weeks, or perhaps months, he felt a satisfaction and completion within himself that had not been there before.

At the same time, just as he had felt after the death of his wife, that he had 'cleared the deck' of everything that was cumbersome, restrictive and clinging, he was ready for action.

But what that entailed he had for the moment no idea.

Chapter Five

THERESA CAME very slowly down the back stairs, not troubling to be quiet because there was nobody to hear her, and let herself out through the garden door.

The dawn had only just broken and she doubted if even the servants were yet awake and going to the kitchen for their first cup of coffee.

They had got to bed surprisingly late the night before, because unexpectedly, almost as if an explosion had occurred, the *Marquis* had come home.

In the three weeks that Theresa had been at the Château Sare, she had been so happy that she had almost forgotten there was a Master of the Château by whom she was employed.

When she had first arrived she had been apprehensive in case, as Gennie feared, the servants were hostile and disagreeable and she would feel humiliated by them.

Instead as they drove from the station through the beautiful wooded country, passing very few cottages on the way, she realised she had stepped into a world that was quite different from anything she had known before.

In the far distance, although she could not see them, she knew there were the Pyrenees and sometimes the wind would blow cold from the mountains, especially in the winter.

To the West, although again she could not see it, there was the sea.

She fancied there was a touch of salt in the air and visualised the rolling ocean stretching from the French coast across the Atlantic to the new worlds of which she knew so little.

Then as they drove through the woods which were bursting with the green leaves of Spring, she had her first sight of the Château.

It was so beautiful, so fairy-like, so like something out of her imagination, that she drew in her breath and could only stare at it thinking it was unreal.

Later, when she knew it better, she found that everything about it was a delight, from the formal gardens laid out in the pattern set by Louis XIV, to the great State Rooms that had been designed and decorated at the same time, and which had changed very little with the passing years.

Because Château Sare was so far away from Paris and several miles from the nearest market-town, it had escaped the horrors of the Revolution and the ravages of the Napoleonic Wars, like a precious jewel enclosed and safely preserved among its woods.

It was to be discovered now, Theresa thought, only by people who were really interested, and that was what she became, more and more so every day.

All the servants at the Château were very old, and had been there for years.

Once they got over their surprise of finding that the new Chef was not only a woman but also very young, they treated her as if she was a child whom they must protect and look after.

They were only too willing to do anything she asked of them, and they tried to prevent her from working, not because they were jealous or looked on her as an intruder, but because they felt it might be too much for her.

In actual fact, she found there was very little for her to do.

The servants were all one big family and there was an elderly man who had cooked for them at the Château for thirty years, whose food was very much to their liking. The two scullions who turned the big spits in the great kitchen, emptied the rubbish and brought in the wood and coal for the fire, were her two grandsons.

They were the only young people besides Theresa in the whole Château. The two boys joked with each other but were on the whole well behaved and too frightened not to obey their grandmother.

Theresa soon after she arrived baked them delicious *pâtisseries* oozing with fruit and cream, and from that moment they were her slaves and there was nothing they would not do to be rewarded with another *pâtisserie.*

She soon settled into a very easy routine.

She cooked for herself and Gennie and they ate together alone in what had been the Steward's Room, which was on the other side of the flagged passage from the great kitchen.

The rest of the household ate in the kitchen as they had always done, and were relieved that they did not have to be on their best behaviour because she was with them.

As *Monsieur* Brantome had promised, Theresa and Gennie had their own Sitting-Room, and the *Maître d'Hôtel* had not given them bedrooms in what were the servants' quarters.

Instead they were in what Theresa knew were the secondary guest rooms provided for visitors of no particular social importance.

He had explained this by saying that the Chef's Room in the past had always been where the men-servants slept.

But Theresa felt certain it was really because the old man instinctively felt that she did not really belong to the servant class.

Nothing however was said, but with the tact that was characteristic of the French, everything was arranged so smoothly and without comment that such favouritism was accepted by everybody in the Château.

It was certainly very much to Gennie's liking.

"We are lucky to have such pretty rooms and such comfortable ones," Theresa remarked.

"It would be better if you were staying here as yourself, M'Lady!"

"But I am not!" Theresa said sharply. "And do remember, Gennie, that I am the Chef, *Mademoiselle* Beauvais, and I shall be very angry if through you the others become suspicious that I am not who I say I am."

Theresa knew that Gennie thought they were suspicious already but had decided there was no point in arguing. She was in fact delighted with their accommodation and the attention the other servants were giving Theresa and herself.

The morning after their arrival Theresa had baked some croissants for their breakfast.

These they had enjoyed with golden butter from the *Marquis*'s own cows, honey from his own bee-hives, and coffee which was improved with thick cream also from the Home Farm.

After this, Gennie went upstairs to unpack while Theresa decided to explore.

She went out into the sunshine, just as she was without a bonnet, and it was warm enough to need no wrap over her thin gown.

The gardens were a delight, and she wondered how anybody except an insensitive man like her father, and obviously the *Marquis*, could prefer Paris to their exquisite beauty.

There were fountains throwing their water iridescent up towards the sky, there were pools in which swam large golden carp, and already the lilac and syringa were in bloom, scenting the air.

Tulips, hyacinths and daffodils abounded, and it was all so lovely that she felt as she had when she had first walked into the Château that she was in Fairyland.

She moved through the garden and opened a door in an ancient wall, thinking beyond it she would find an orchard with the trees in blossom. Indeed, it was so and the pink and white petals were falling on the grass like snowflakes.

Then suddenly she stood very still, thinking that what she was seeing could not be real. Just ahead of her, in a large enclosure were a lion and a lioness.

She went nearer to them holding her breath because she was so excited.

They were lying together side by side under the trees and as she approached them the lion raised his head to look at her.

As if he decided she was not of any great importance he lowered it again onto his outstretched front paws.

Theresa then looked further to where she saw almost as if in a dream another enclosure and she thought there was another beyond that.

The animals were free to roam within the confines of their own particular territory and Theresa realised with a leap of her heart that she was seeing for the first time in her life a private Menagerie.

It was something that had always interested her because she loved animals and she walked on to find there was an enclosure containing a pair of zebras next to the lions.

She stood looking at them for a long time, knowing they were exactly what she had imagined zebras would be like and just as incredible.

There was another enclosure which was even larger, and this contained a number of different types of antelope and deer.

She was watching them moving with an inexpressible grace beneath the trees when in front of some artificial rocks at the far end of the enclosure there appeared to her delight a young giraffe.

With his long neck and ungainly legs he looked so strange that she clasped her hands together and gave a little laugh.

Then a voice behind her made her jump.

"You find him amusing, *M'mselle?*"

Theresa turned her head to see an old man with white hair looking at her in surprise.

"Bonjour, Monsieur!"

"Bonjour, M'mselle! I am not quite certain you should be here, because this is private property."

"I only arrived yesterday evening," Theresa explained, "and I am the new Chef."

The old man looked at her as if he thought she was mocking him.

She gave a little laugh as she insisted:

"Yes, I am the Chef, although I am a woman, and look so young! Now tell me about these marvellous and exciting animals."

It was the beginning of a close friendship, for Jacques, as the old man was called, had looked after the *Marquis*'s Menagerie ever since it had been first been formed.

He told Theresa how when the *Marquis* was a very young boy and had gone around the world, he had brought back three animals with him.

The first was so exciting that Theresa could only look and go on looking and feel she would never have time for any of the others.

'A Maharajah in India arranged a tiger-shoot for *Monsieur le Marquis*," he explained, "but when he killed his first tigress he found she had one small cub which was only about a week old, and no bigger than a kitten. *Monsieur* fed it himself with goat's milk, and by the time he arrived home it had grown quite large, and it followed *Monsieur* everywhere as if it was a dog."

Looking at the tiger now, which was sitting in an enclosure beyond the lions, Theresa thought he was the most marvellous animal she had ever seen in her whole life.

She could see the markings on his face, the brightness of his eyes, and when he yawned as if her scrutiny bored him, she was aware of his long, sharp, pointed teeth which were made to kill.

"He is magnificent!" she exclaimed, knowing that Jacques was waiting to hear what she thought of such a superior animal.

"*Monsieur* gave him the right name," Jacques commented with a smile.

"What is it?" Theresa asked curiously.

"Le Roi!"

"But of course," Theresa cried. "What could be more appropriate? King of the Jungle, King of the Beasts! That is exactly what he looks like as he lies there, a King, thinking we should all bow to him, and if we do not do so, he will make us!"

"Only *Monsieur le Marquis* can handle him," Jacques said. "He tolerates me, but no one else dares go onto his ground which he guards because it is his, and his alone."

Almost as if he thought they were impertinent to be discussing him, the tiger rose and deliberately turned his back on Theresa and Jacques, and lay down.

Now she could see his fine dark markings from the top of his head to the tip of his tail.

Jacques showed her the other animals they had in the Menagerie, but although she was interested, Theresa's thoughts kept returning to *'Le Roi'*.

"Once we had many more," Jacques said beside her a little sadly, "but they grew old and died, and *Monsieur* is not as interested in them as he used to be."

For the first time since she had come to the Château Theresa's lips tightened.

She knew exactly why *Monsieur le Marquis* was no longer interested in his animals or his beautiful home.

It was because like her father he was fascinated, infatuated and bewitched by women who kept him in Paris.

That night when she went to bed she thought about *Le Roi* and was certain that as he was the only animal in his enclosure and without a companion he must be lonely.

She thought it was typical, and what she would expect of the *Marquis*, to make the tiger-cub love him, then as he grew older to abandon him as he doubtless abandoned a woman, without a thought for his suffering.

When she awoke early the next morning, almost instinctively her feet carried her through the garden and out through the door in the wall.

She saw the lions were sleeping close together and made straight for the tiger's cage.

Because she had been so much alone at the Dower House

and had nobody of her own age with whom she could play, Theresa had automatically tried to attract the deer in the Park, the birds in the trees, and even the rabbits.

When she was very small her mother had read her the story of St. Francis of Assisi who was always surrounded by the beasts of the forest and the birds in the air.

She told her how he called to them and preached to them as they sat around him in perfect harmony with each other and listened.

It was something she wanted to do too.

She had read how the magic of the Gypsies' 'way with animals' was a secret which they divulged to no one except those of their own blood.

But she had reasoned it out for herself that first an animal had to feel safe, and he could only feel safe if the vibrations of the person trying to attract him were those of love.

Theresa had tried to communicate her love first to the birds, and as she fed them at the same time they gradually became so used to her that they would fly down onto her shoulders when she sat beneath a tree.

Then they would eat the crumbs she had brought them from her hand, and even when the crumbs were not there they would sit looking at her with their sharp little eyes as if they knew they could trust her.

She was just as successful with the deer which had roamed wild in the Park for centuries.

The spotted deer were the most difficult to tame, but soon they came when she called them and would allow her to touch them, and even the stags trusted her.

She thought now of the way she talked to her horses so that even the wildest and most obstreperous of them would behave well when she was riding it.

Sitting down outside *Le Roi*'s pen she began to talk to him, and she was sure it must have been something the *Marquis* had done when the lion was a cub.

At first he appeared to ignore the softness of her voice and the coaxing manner in which she begged him to come nearer.

But after a few days she knew he was watching for her first

thing in the morning, and in the afternoon when Gennie would put her feet up after luncheon and have a short snooze.

It was then that Theresa would hurry into the garden, drawn like a magnet to *Le Roi.*

By the end of the week he was not only waiting for her but she could touch him through the iron railings.

Jacques had given her very strict instructions.

"You are never, *M'mselle*, never to go into *Le Roi*'s cage! Now that he is old he is not safe, and although he would never touch *Monsieur* he has twice attacked the boys who help me feed the animals and clean out their cages. Now I am the only person who goes inside, except of course the Master."

He paused before he added:

"But I am careful, very careful, never to turn my back on *Le Roi.* No tiger is really trustworthy."

Theresa did not believe him. She was sure that once *Le Roi* knew how much she loved him he would respond to her love and would never hurt her.

She was not surprised that Gennie was not in the slightest interested in the Menagerie.

"I've no time for animals," she said, "especially those that are dangerous. You be careful, M'Lady, you don't want scars on your pretty face and a couple of fingers bitten off!"

Theresa laughed.

"I will be very careful, Gennie, and there is no chance of that."

"You never know!" Gennie said darkly. "If you ask me, lions and such-like should be left where they belong, and not brought to what to them is foreign parts."

"That is the argument people have always used against Zoos," Theresa remarked, "but man has been attracted to wild animals since the beginning of time."

Gennie was not interested, and Theresa found herself longing to talk with somebody more knowledgeable about the history of animals being kept in captivity.

Jacques did not love those he tended, and was only

carrying out his orders. As she found when they talked together he had never read a book because he could not read.

There was so much she wanted to know that she went into the large Library and opened the wooden shutters to see if she could find anything which would enlighten her further.

The Library was fantastic! She had never seen so many books collected together under an exquisitely painted ceiling. But she felt it might take her months and months to find the ones she wanted.

"Is there no Curator who looks after the books and all the treasures?" she asked the *Maître d'Hôtel.*

"There was one, *M'mselle,*" he answered in his quavering voice, "but he died two years ago, since when *Monsieur* Brantome has not sent us another."

He gave a short laugh that turned into a cough before he added:

"If somebody came I'm sure they'd be like the Chefs who never stay because it's so lonely here."

"I think it is marvellous!" Theresa said. "How could one be lonely with so many treasures to look at, such beautiful gardens, and of course the animals?"

The *Maître d'Hôtel* laughed again.

"You're different from anybody who has come to us before, *M'mselle*, and we're all hoping you'll not leave too soon."

"I never want to leave here!"

She smiled at him, but as she walked away through the open door into the sunshine she did not realise that he was shaking his head as if he thought that like a young bird, she would sooner or later want to spread her wings.

Theresa however was entranced with everything she saw and everything she did, but most of all with *Le Roi.*

She had been at the Château for ten days when, her heart beating quickly at her own daring, one afternoon she opened the door to *Le Roi*'s enclosure and entered it.

She knew it was the right time to make such an experiment because he had been fed at midday by Jacques and would not be in an aggressive mood.

At the same time Jacques had impressed upon her so often that *Le Roi* was dangerous, that she knew she was doing what he would think exceedingly reprehensible.

She shut the door behind her and stood very still. Then she called *Le Roi* very softly in the same coaxing tone she always used to him.

Slowly he rose to his feet, every muscle moving with a rhythmical grace under his thick fur.

Then without hurrying he came towards her, and Theresa was aware it was the moment when if he wished to, he could spring upon her, force her to the ground, and probably kill her.

Instead as he came to her side he did not pause, but rubbed himself gently against her leg.

As he did so he was purring in his throat as a cat might do, and she knew she had won.

******

The *Marquis* arrived at the Halt where the trains could be stopped for anybody who was visiting the Château Sare.

He had however given orders that such a privilege was only to be used by himself and his guests and not by the staff.

It had caused quite a commotion in Paris when after finding his coach which had been attached to the Express going South he informed the Guard that he wished to stop at the Halt for Château Sare.

"It's a long time, *Monsieur le Marquis*, since I have been asked to do that," the Guard said.

"I know, and I can hear the condemnation in your voice because I have been so tardy in visiting my home," the *Marquis* smiled.

"Your people will be glad to see you, *Monsieur*," the Guard replied, before he hurried away to give the engine-driver his instructions.

The train was a fast one, but the *Marquis* did not arrive at the Château until after eight o'clock.

He had deliberately told Brantome not to inform the staff

of his coming, because he had always insisted that everybody in his various Châteaux should be fully prepared for his arrival at any time and without warning.

It annoyed him to think that in his absence everything might not be kept up to perfection, and he had no idea how much his secretary worried in case an unexpected arrival on the part of his Master might cause innumerable problems.

He had, in fact, said to the *Marquis* the night before he left:

"Allow me, *Monsieur*, to send a message first thing tomorrow morning to the Château warning them to be ready for you. After all, you must be aware, *Monsieur*, that you have not been there for over two years."

"I cannot believe that everything has become as lax as I can see you anticipate," the *Marquis* said sharply. "But if it has, I shall be extremely angry!"

There was nothing more Brantome could do, and he merely prayed that everything would turn out well and that the new Chef had not been lying when she claimed to be a first-class cook.

The *Marquis*'s arrival was in fact as sensational as if lightning had struck the Château.

The *Maître d'Hôtel* had been alerted by the night-footman, who had been dozing in the comfortable padded chair in the hall when the carriage drew up at the door.

Hurrying into his gold braided coat he was breathless by the time he reached his Master who had walked into the Salon.

It was fortunate that the night-footman had remembered to light the candelabra before he left the *Marquis* to summons him for the room was looking exceedingly attractive.

There was, he saw thankfully by the mercy of God, a large bowl of fresh flowers on the Louis Seize table in the window.

This, the *Maître d'Hôtel* knew was entirely due to Theresa.

'The flowers in the garden are so lovely,' she had said. "Do you think I might pick some, not only for my Sitting-Room, but also for the *Grand Salon* which looks somehow neglected without fresh flowers to echo the colours of the tapestry chairs and the pictures by Fragonard."

The Maître d'Hôtel had smiled.

"But of course, *M'mselle*," he said. "When *Madame La Marquise* was alive, she always insisted there should be flowers everywhere, in the Salon, the Library, the Drawing-Rooms, and of course the Dining-table was decorated every evening for dinner."

"It must have looked lovely!"

Because she wanted to picture how it must have looked when *Madame La Marquise*, whose portrait hung in one of the Reception Rooms, was alive, she arranged vases of daffodils, pink camelias and white lilac.

She begged the gardeners, who had ceased to be interested in the inside of the Château, to bring in bowls of hyacinths which filled the hall with their fragrance.

Because like the rest of the staff the gardeners also were old, they were delighted when she praised them for what they had done and she was as excited as a child when they brought her the first peaches from the greenhouses and the first bunch of muscat grapes.

"You are so kind," she cried.

They tried to think of what else they could do to please her, simply because they liked to see her eyes shining with delight and her lips smiling.

They were all so old that she did not think of them as men whom she hated as a sex.

In fact, the *Maître d'Hôtel*, the Head gardener, the Butler, and indeed most of the other men in the house were all old enough to be her grandfather.

Now into what she was finding was like a little Paradise of her own, there had arrived unexpectedly and shatteringly the *Marquis*.

As she hurried to the kitchen to prepare his dinner which she devoutly hoped would please him, she tried not to become agitated but to think quietly and calmly of what late at night after a long journey a gentleman who expected perfection would require.

She was quite certain that in Paris he would have had a surfeit of very rich food and probably too much *pâté de foie gras.*

She was not to know that the previous night not only had he had a surfeit of that dish, but also of caviare from Russia, quails from Africa, and truffles which to a Frenchman was an essential delicacy that no good meal could lack.

Almost as if she was clairvoyant Theresa thought perhaps the *Marquis* had come home to suddenly from Paris because he was bored with the exotic orgies which had so delighted her father.

'Why else would he seek the country?' she echoed.

She was sure it was not because he was short of money as her father had been.

She therefore decided to put away any idea of surprising him with any of her more complicated and sophisticated dishes which her grandmother had taught her and which were for very special occasions.

Instead she started with a *consommé* so clear, so golden, and so delicious that every mouthful was a delight.

By a stroke of good fortune, one of the game-keepers who was anxious to please her had brought in two freshly caught trout that very evening.

"I thought, *M'mselle,*" he said respectfully, "you'd like to taste our trout which we've always believed have a better flavour than any other fish in the whole neighbourhood."

Theresa had smiled at the pride in his voice and thanked him, planning to cook the trout for herself and Gennie for luncheon the following day.

Now as a second course she cooked them for the *Marquis* quite simply in butter, only at the last moment garnishing them with a few almonds.

Then there was a choice of either baby lamb which had come from the Home Farm two days earlier, to which the *Maître d'Hôtel* was very partial, or a chicken.

This was to have been eaten by the rest of the household for their midday meal the next day.

She chose the baby lamb, cooking it as her grandmother

had taught her to do with pepper and just a touch of garlic, with no sauce except for its own juices, the meat pink in the middle.

When it was ready she knew it was so tender that it was as soft as velvet.

She was sure that the *Marquis* would not want cheese, which in France always came before the dessert, so late in the evening, but she prepared a *crêpe suzette,* adding orange curaçao and a touch of cognac as her grandmother had shown her.

By the time the *Marquis* was ready it looked most delectable in a silver dish with the Sare coat-of-arms emblazoned on it.

Gennie in the meantime had prepared some new potatoes to serve with the baby lamb and the first peas from the garden, which were so small it seemed almost cruel to take them from the pod.

On another plate she arranged half-a-dozen juicy green asparagus tips.

"If he is not satisfied with the meal," Theresa said to Gennie as they left the kitchen, "there is nothing better I can do at a moment's notice."

Nevertheless as they went up to their own rooms she hoped first that the *Marquis* would be pleased with what he had eaten, and secondly that he would not make too many enquiries about the Chef.

He had not said so, but she felt the *Maître d'Hôtel* would not have informed his Master immediately upon his arrival that there was a new Chef at the Château.

She had discovered that no fewer than six Chefs had come and gone since the *Marquis*'s last visit, and in fact for two months before her arrival there had been no Chef at all.

"We just hoped that *Monsieur* would not come home," one of the women told her. "He would have been very angry and perhaps would have said it was our fault that the Chefs would not stay."

She had paused to add in an affronted voice:

"They were arrogant, *M'mselle*, you have no idea how

arrogant they were! 'Call this living?' one of them said. 'You are all dead and in the grave.' Then he went upstairs and packed his box for Paris!"

Theresa had laughed, but the woman said bitterly:

"He was a man, and all any Frenchman wants to do is to go to Paris!"

She went to bed still wondering whether the *Marquis* was pleased with what he had eaten.

Theresa had slept peacefully, awakening with the knowledge that if she wanted to see *Le Roi* she would have to do so very early before his Master was awake.

She was determined to keep out of the *Marquis*'s way and reasoned to herself that she must stay in her own part of the Château until he left.

It would be very hard not to ride his horses as she had been doing every day, because the Head Groom, another old man, had sensed that she was longing to ride and had actually suggested it.

After he had seen her way with a horse he had let her choose any one she pleased from the stable, and she had not only ridden them around the Park but also over the jumps on the race-course.

This had been built, she learnt, for the *Marquis* when he was a young man.

The jumps were quite high, but since they presented no difficulty for Theresa the Head Groom encouraged her to take the horses, one by one, over them.

"It's what I should be doing every day myself, *M'mselle,*" he said, "but I've had rheumatism in my legs this winter, and it's giving me terrible pains which'll only get better when the warm weather comes."

Theresa was only too delighted to ride the horses, but even so, the most exciting time of the day was when she could be with *Le Roi.*

Now he would let her put her arms around him and would lie on his back for her to scratch his chest, nuzzling against her when she stopped in the same way that Rover did.

Rover who went everywhere at her heels, was very jealous

of *Le Roi* and when she explained he could not go into the enclosure but had to wait for her outside, he at first whimpered.

Then he realised there was something else very exciting to occupy him while his mistress was engaged and that was to explore the rabbit-holes.

He obviously became determined with a will-power that had something human about it, to catch one of the rabbits, however deep into the ground it had hidden itself.

He burrowed down, his nose covered with mud, and he almost wore the claws of his front paws away. But although he knew the rabbits were there and could smell them, he never managed to catch one.

Theresa therefore only had to call him when she left *Le Roi* and he was at her heels.

When she went riding he ran beside her horse, getting all the exercise he needed in keeping up.

"I am so happy," Theresa said to herself almost every night, "because I am safe."

Her fear of her Uncle had receded into the distance and she very seldom thought of him.

Her only sadness was that her mother could not be with her, and yet she was sure she knew and was glad that she was in France, and living in the sort of Château that had belonged to the Chaufours.

The first golden rays of the sun were moving up the horizon and the last evening star was fading away as Thesesa opened *Le Roi*'s enclosure and slipped inside.

He came bounding towards her and she said to him:

"*Bonjour, bonjour, Le Roi!* I have something very exciting to tell you: your Master has arrived, and I know you will be delighted to see him."

She walked to where the ground rose a little and sat down under a tree that was in blossom.

She began to scratch *Le Roi* behind the ears which he loved, and when he settled down closer to her as she did so, she felt that he was listening as she went on:

"I shall not be able to come to see you as often as I would

like, now that your Master is here, but I shall be loving you and thinking about you. If it is safe, I will come very early in the morning, like now, when there is nobody about."

Quite suddenly she put her arms around the tiger's neck and put her head against the softness of his fur as she said:

"I love you, *Le Roi!* Promise me you will not forget me, or love your Master so much that you stop loving me."

She felt as if the great animal understood and responded to the love she was giving him.

Then as she pulled him even closer to her with the intensity of her feelings, she looked up.

Standing just inside the gate with a look of sheer astonishment on his face was a man.

It was the *Marquis*!

Chapter Six

FOR A moment Theresa was frozen into immobility.

Then *Le Roi* raised his head and rising moved quickly towards the *Marquis.*

When he reached him the tiger stood up on his hind legs and put his paws on the *Marquis*'s shoulders so that they were face to face.

For a few seconds man and beast looked at each other, then *Le Roi* got down on the ground and rubbed himself affectionately against the *Marquis*'s legs.

Theresa had risen to her feet and now feeling uncertain and embarrassed she moved towards the *Marquis*, aware there was no other way for her to leave the enclosure except by the gate behind him.

As she reached him he asked angrily:

"How did you get in here? Surely you must be aware this animal is dangerous?"

Theresa smiled.

"Not to me, *Monsieur*."

"Who are you?"

Too late Theresa realised she should have curtsied, and she made a small obeisance before she replied:

"I am your new Chef, *Monsieur*."

Now the *Marquis*'s eyebrows seemed to rise up on his square forehead almost as if to touch his dark hair.

"My new Chef?" he repeated as if he must reassure himself of what he had heard.

Then after a perceptible pause he added:

"Then you cooked the dinner I ate last night!"

"Yes, *Monsieur*."

His eyes flicked over her and she knew he was taking in her slim figure in the simple muslin gown she wore.

She was also aware that she looked younger than usual because having risen so early she had not arranged her hair at all elaborately but had just swept it back from her forehead into a coil at the nape of her neck.

She was sure, as if the *Marquis* had spoken aloud, that he was wondering, as *Monsieur* Brantome had, if this was some sort of joke thought up by his friends.

Then as Theresa took a step towards the gate behind him the *Marquis* said:

"Wait! I want to talk to you, and perhaps you will tell me why you should risk your life by coming in here with *Le Roi*."

Theresa replied without thinking:

"He seemed lonely, *Monsieur*, the only animal in an enclosure by himself. I thought too that you had deserted him."

As she spoke Theresa felt she had made a terrible mistake in being so frank. Yet the words had come spontaneously to her lips and she answered as she would have to a question put to her by her mother.

"What is your name?"

The question was sharp, and she suspected this was a characteristic way the *Marquis* had of speaking.

"Theresa . . .Beauvais."

She hesitated over the surname, being so upset that the *Marquis* had discovered her with *Le Roi*, that she had almost said 'Holme'.

"Then perhaps you will tell me, *Mademoiselle* Beauvais," the *Marquis* said, "how it is that at your age you know how to control wild animals, above all a tiger, which is probably the most unpredictable of them all."

Theresa was about to tell the truth and simply say that she gave him love.

Then she remembered she was speaking to a man who would doubtless misinterpret such an explanation.

As she thought about the *Marquis* as her employer and as *Le Roi*'s master, she remembered he was a man who had come from Paris!

Without consciously realising it, her whole body stiffened and the expression in her large eyes changed.

The *Marquis*, who was very perceptive, was immediately aware that she was now looking at him not shyly as she had done when he had first spoken to her, but with an obvious dislike.

And yet Theresa could not help thinking that he was exceedingly handsome in a very unusual way.

His dark hair, brushed back from his square forehead, his clear-cut features and his dark eyebrows would in England have made him immediately recognisable as a foreigner.

At the same time she was surprised by the sharp expression in his eyes.

He was looking at her as if he was probing beneath the surface, as if he had penetrated her disguise and sought the truth.

Because she had no wish to talk to him more than was unavoidable she said:

"As you are up early, *Monsieur*, I must return to the Château to cook your breakfast."

"There is plenty of time for that," the *Marquis* replied, "and you have not yet answered my question. How can you have become so intimate with *Le Roi*, unless of course you have worked with wild animals before you came here. Perhaps in a Circus?''

It was such a funny idea that Theresa laughed.

''No, *Monsieur*, nothing so romantic! Actually I had never even seen a live tiger before I met *Le Roi*.''

''In which case,'' the *Marquis* said, ''how can you take such a risk as to come into this enclosure, knowing that you might be mauled, if not killed?''

Because he was obviously waiting for her to answer Theresa felt compelled to reply:

''I talked to *Le Roi* until I knew I could trust him.''

''You talked to him? What are you saying? Have you some magic formula, such as the gypsies have which will make an animal obey you?''

Theresa was surprised that he knew about the gypsies and she gave him a quick glance before she said:

''I have always longed to know the gypsy magic. Actually, I do not think it is words that count with animals, but the tone of one's voice, and of course the vibrations one sends towards them.''

She was thinking of the birds as she spoke and was unaware as she did so that she glanced up at the trees overhead.

''So you have done this before,'' the *Marquis* said. ''In all the years that *Le Roi* has belonged to me I have never known him allow anybody else to touch him.''

As they were talking *Le Roi* was still rubbing himself against the *Marquis* who was now scratching him behind the ears in the way Theresa knew he loved.

She looked at the tiger and her eyes softened.

''He is so beautiful!'' she said. ''How could you bear to go for two years without seeing him?''

It was a question she had asked herself so often that it now came involuntarily to her lips.

Then because she knew the answer, she felt the anger which always rose in her at the thought of Paris surging through her breast until, with her eyes still on *Le Roi*, she added:

"How could any . . body in Paris be more beautiful than he is? Or anything in that horrible, degrading place be as attractive as this Château?"

The words seemed to come from her lips uncontrollably.

Then as if she realised what she had said and knew she could not explain or apologise for it, she pulled open the gate which the *Marquis* had closed, slipped through it, and ran as quickly as she could towards the door in the wall.

She was breathless by the time she reached the Château and she hurried upstairs to find Gennie had just finished dresssing and was fastening a white apron round her waist.

"So you are up, M'Lady!" she exclaimed. "I was just coming to call you. I thought we should be early this morning in case *Monsieur le Marquis*, although I very much doubt it, is an early riser."

"He is already up," Theresa answered, "and I am going down to the kitchen."

The words seemed to jerk themselves out of her lips, and she was aware that Gennie looked at her in surprise before, having no wish to answer any more questions, she ran towards the stairs which led to the kitchen-quarters.

The servants were just beginning to stir themselves and she had a glimpse of the Butler and footmen in the Pantry.

One of the older women was starting to scrub the flag-stones along the passage which led past the kitchen towards the back yard.

Before she went to bed last night, she had put everything ready to bake the *croissants* which she expected the *Marquis* would require for his *petit déjeuner*.

Now, she thought, as he was up so early, he might be hungry, and just to surprise him she would give him an English breakfast.

Working quickly with the skill her grandmother had taught her, she prepared a number of dishes that her mother always ordered when her father was at home.

There were different dishes of eggs, one of kedgeree, another of mushrooms which the gardeners brought into the kitchen while she was cooking and there were chickens' legs left over from luncheon the day before which she devilled with a special sauce.

She put everything into crested silver entrée dishes and was relieved to find they had lighted candles beneath them which kept them hot.

She had no idea whether the *Marquis* would enjoy such a breakfast, but she had the feeling that because he was curious it would not be very long before she saw him again.

She had just finished the last dish, and the coffee pot was bubbling on the stove, when the *Maître d'Hôtel* sent a message to say:

"*Monsieur* is ready for his *petit déjeuner.*"

"Not so *'petit'* today!" Theresa wanted to reply.

At the same time, she was apprehensive that the *Marquis* might be angry first at her having gone into *Le Roi*'s enclosure, and secondly because of the impertinent way she had spoken to him.

"Why did I not just say: *'Oui, Monsieur'*, and *'Non, Monsieur'*? Theresa asked herself angrily.

She had not really considered what she would do if she should meet the *Marquis*, but it was certainly not to talk to him as she had.

If she had thought about him at all, it had been with hatred because he was in the same category, she told herself, as her father.

Ever since she had come to the Château she had despised him for leaving his animals and his home to waste his time with women like Jeanne Tourbey.

Doubtless too he had spent a fortune decking them out in furs and jewellery.

"He is despicable!" she told herself.

She had been so glad that in his absence she could play with *Le Roi*, and ride his horses that the man himself had gradually faded from her thoughts.

Now as she cooked she was vividly conscious of him.

She knew that he had a very strong personality and it was impossible to dismiss him as a useless seeker after pleasure, as she wanted to do.

Then almost like a knife in her heart she suddenly feared that because she had been impertinent he would dismiss her.

"If he does that, where shall we go?" she asked.

She knew it would be an agony she had never expected to leave the Château.

She took the *croissants* and coffee she and Gennie were having, to the room where they ate alone.

As she opened the door she found to her surprise that Gennie was standing talking to a strange man.

She came quickly to the door, almost pushing Theresa outside it as she said in a whisper:

"Go along the passage, you're not eating in here!"

"Why not?" Theresa asked.

"Because this is where *Monsieur*'s valet will eat. We can use the small Writing Room."

"What is this about?" Theresa asked.

"I arranged it with the *Maître d'Hôtel*," Gennie replied. "I spoke to him last night, and he understood."

Theresa was still looking doubtful as she said:

"It's not right that you should be sitting down with valets and such-like. He'll be familiar, and then what could you do about it?"

Without saying so, Theresa realised that the *Marquis*'s valet must be a young man.

She therefore allowed Gennie to take the tray from her, and they went into what had once been a Writing Room, where the guests could have a place where they were not disturbed when they had an important letter to write.

It was tastefully furnished with a large, important-looking desk, and there was a round table on which they could eat.

Theresa appreciated that it was in fact far more attractive than the room they had used previously.

She was just finishing her coffee when the *Maître d'Hôtel* came to the door to say:

"*Monsieur le Marquis* wishes to speak to you, *M'mselle* Beauvais!"

Theresa felt her heart give a frightened throb, but she asked:

"Where will I find him?"

"In his own special room, where *Monsieur* always sits when he's alone. It is next to the Library."

Feeling like a Schoolgirl about to be reprimanded, Theresa walked along the passage towards the Library which was on the other side of the Château.

She had found out which was the *Marquis*'s special room when she had first explored the whole place, and had thought it very attractive with several fine bookcases and a number of pictures of horses which gave it a very masculine look.

As she entered the room the *Marquis* was sitting at a very ornate Louis XIV desk, but he rose and moved to stand in front of the fireplace which Theresa noticed with satisfaction had already been filled with flowers as it was too warm for a fire.

She knew the gardeners must have arranged it very early, and she had the idea that by noon all the rooms the *Marquis* was likely to use would have big vases of flowers in them as she had always wanted.

Now she was very conscious that he was watching her walk what seemed a long distance towards him.

After she had curtsied she said:

"You wished to see me, *Monsieur*?"

"Suppose you sit down, *Mademoiselle* Beauvais?"

He indicated a chair which was exquisitely embroidered in *petit point* and Theresa seated herself a little nervously on the edge of it.

She glanced up at the *Marquis* and unexpectedly he smiled.

"Now," he said, "suppose you tell me what this is all about, and if you are here as a result of a wager or as some publicity stunt which will inevitably find its way into the newspapers."

Theresa stiffened.

"There is nothing like that, *Monsieur*!"

"Then why are you masquerading as a Chef?"

"If my cooking does not please you, *Monsieur*, I can of course only apologise and leave."

"You are perfectly aware that it would be impossible to

find fault with the meal you served me last night," the *Marquis* replied, "or the very English breakfast that I have just enjoyed!"

She was surprised that he realised that it was English, but she looked at him for a moment questioningly and he said:

"I have learned from the *Maître d'Hôtel* that you and your assistant were in England before you came to France."

Theresa did not reply.

She realised it was inevitable that the servants would have asked questions of Gennie, and there was no point in her being untruthful.

"I am waiting."

"I have nothing to tell you, *Monsieur*."

"You can hardly expect me to be satisfied with that! Then let us start from the beginning. Why should you wish to be here, hidden away in what, I am quite certain, is the most obscure and isolated Château in the whole of France, unless there is a very good reason for it."

"The reason is quite simple, *Monsieur*. I wanted employment, and when I showed your secretary, *Monsieur* Brantome, my references he engaged me immediately."

"He told you the sort of place you were coming to?"

"It was exactly what I wanted," Theresa said. "I like being in the country, and I had certainly no wish to be in Paris."

Despite herself her voice hardened and sharpened, and after a moment the *Marquis* asked quietly:

"What has Paris done to you, to make you speak like that?"

"I have only been in Paris for one night."

"Then how did you know my secretary was looking for a Chef?"

"A lady with whom I was travelling in the train from Calais told me you often required Chefs for your Châteaux."

"Do you know the lady's name?"

"Celeste St. Clair."

There was just a flicker to show that the *Marquis* knew of

whom she was speaking, but it was enough to tell her that Celeste St. Clair had been striking at him in some way she did not understand.

"So it was Celeste St. Clair who suggested to you that you might come to me. Do you know her well?"

Theresa shook her head.

"No, *Monsieur.* We only happened to be travelling in the same railway carriage together to Paris."

"But you have been at my Château now for three weeks. I am sure you find it lonely."

It was almost as if he wanted her to agree, but Theresa replied quickly:

"I have loved every second I have been here. It is the most beautiful place I have ever seen! So please, *Monsieur*, allow me to stay."

"Indefinitely?"

"For ever!"

He stared at her. Then he said:

"Surely you cannot be serious. You are young and attractive. Why should you have such an aversion to Paris? And why should any young woman with a face like yours want to bury herself with a lot of old servants who have one foot in the grave?"

He paused as if waiting for Theresa to reply and she thought quickly of what she should say.

"I have told you that I am very happy here, *Monsieur*," she said, "and so is my assistant."

"And I suppose also your dog!"

Theresa had carefully left Rover with Gennie, hoping that the *Marquis* would not be aware that he existed.

Now she remembered that when she had run away from *Le Roi*'s enclosure Rover had come from under the trees where he had been digging into another rabbit-hole and had followed her through the door in the wall.

"He is a very good little dog," she said quickly.

"Of course it is only fair, *Mademoiselle*, that you should have your animals, as I have mine!"

Theresa looked up at him uncomfortable and he said:

"Perhaps you are right about *Le Roi.* He certainly seemed very pleased to see me."

She did not speak and after a moment he went on:

"I have been taken to task for many short-comings in the past, *Mademoiselle* Beauvais, but this is the first time it has been over the neglect of a tiger!"

Theresa thought he was mocking at her and she said quickly:

"I am certain that if one rears an animal from the time it is born, it looks on you as it's real parent. It feels you are its father or mother, or both, and expects the same devotion and the same love. I know that is how a foal I reared felt about me when its mother died."

"And where is that foal now?" the *Marquis* enquired.

"In England."

"And you left him?"

"There was . . nothing else I . . could do."

She could not help a sudden tremor of pain in her voice as she remembered how hard it had been to say goodbye to the horses.

They had been her only companions when she and her mother lived so quietly at the Dower House after her father had left, and especially when her mother was ill.

"I suspect, although I have not been told so," the *Marquis* remarked, "that you have been riding my horses since you arrived here."

Again Theresa was looking at him and now, although she was not aware of it, pleadingly.

"I have helped to exercise them, *Monsieur*," she replied, "and I have taken them over the jumps every day."

"Surely you found them rather high?"

Theresa shook her head.

"No, the horses are used to the height, so I think they should be raised a little."

Quite unexpectedly the *Marquis* put his head back and laughed.

Theresa looked at him in surprise and he said:

"I just do not believe this is happening! I come home after

a regrettably long absence to find that a young woman, who tells me she is my Chef, has tamed my otherwise ferocious tiger, is riding my horses, and doubtless has been making a number of innovations on my Estate which will be revealed in due course!"

Theresa clasped her hands together.

"I am sorry, *Monsieur,* if you think it is a great impertinence, but you were not here and everybody seemed to think they were forgotten and it has been so . . wonderful for . . me."

"And you really think such a life will content you for long?"

"I am sure of it!"

"Then of course, *Mademoiselle*, I can only give you my blessing, and say in the Eastern manner that everything I have is yours!"

"You mean I can go on riding?"

"If it pleases you."

"And you will not put *Le Roi* against me?"

The *Marquis* laughed.

"I am not going to advise you to take care, because I think there is no need for it."

Theresa smiled.

"I think *Le Roi* trusts me, and I am very, very grateful, *Monsieur*, that you too should do so."

As if she thought the interview had come to an end she rose to her feet, but the *Marquis* said:

"You have still not given me an explanation as to why you have come from England."

She did not answer and after a moment he said:

"Very well, I will not press you, and if the safety of the Château is what you need, then I do not think you will find a better place in which to hide."

Theresa started at the last words, and when she looked at him she realised he had said it deliberately to see her reaction.

There seemed no point in pretending.

"Yes, I am hiding," she said, "and I do feel safe here."

"I suppose it would be quite useless," the *Marquis* said, "to ask you to trust me and tell me why you are frightened?"

Theresa shook her head as he went on:

"Or why you hate Paris."

Because she was so grateful to him for not pressing her to tell him why she was hiding, Theresa said:

"For one reason, because I think that, as the Venetians did, the French are destroying themselves in their pursuit of pleasure. They seem completely oblivious to the fact that the enemy is at their gate and they might, at any time, be overwhelmed."

She spoke in the same way that she might have replied to a question from her mother.

Only as she finished speaking did she realise that the *Marquis* had stiffened and was staring at her now with narrowed eyes.

"Why are you saying that?" he asked sharply. "Who told you that the enemy was at the gate?"

The colour rose in Theresa's face.

"I have been living in England," she said, "but my mother had the French newspapers sent to her every week. I read them all from *'Le Jour'* down to the very revolutionary ones."

"And what did you gather from what you read?"

Because she had said so much, it seemed a mistake not to tell him now what he obviously wanted to hear.

"My mother was certain of two things," Theresa replied. "First, that the Prussians intend sooner or later to fight France and humiliate her. Secondly, that the unrest among the abominably paid French working people sooner or later will explode into what might be another revolution."

She spoke defiantly because as she answered the question she thought that the *Marquis*, like her father, was frittering away his time and his money with women when he should be concerned with the dangerous situation of his country.

Her eyes, as she met his, had darkened contemptuously.

For a moment the *Marquis* was obviously too surprised to answer. Then he said:

"How could you possibly know such things when you were in England?"

"I told you, *Monsieur*, we read the newspapers, and

although my mother was out of touch with her relatives in France she had a perception that was almost like clairvoyance about the country she loved."

"And you feel the same?"

"I only know that I hate Paris with its wild extravagance and its refusal to face the truth," Theresa said.

Then, as if she felt she must finish what she had begun, she added:

"Now you understand why I want to stay here where there is nothing to soil the beauty that comes from God."

There was a little tremor in her voice as she thought of how her father had tarnished not only everything that was good, but also her mother's prayers.

To her surprise the *Marquis* sat down in the chair beside her and said quietly:

"Who has hurt you? Who has made you hate so violently everything that happens in Paris? Was it a man?"

Like a startled fawn Theresa jumped to her feet.

"It is something I do not wish to talk about, *Monsieur*," she said. "I am sure it is incorrect for you to question me, as one of your servants, and as I have work to do, will you please excuse me?"

She did not look at him but merely curtsied and hurried towards the door.

Only as she reached it did the *Marquis* say sharply:

"Wait, *Mademoiselle!*"

Reluctantly, even as she turned the handle, she stopped to find that he had risen to stand looking at her.

"We have not yet finished our conversation," he said. "Since it is something which interests me, I will allow you to go now, to attend to your work, but I wish to talk to you again later in the day. Is that understood?"

Theresa drew in her breath.

She wanted to argue with him, to tell him that her place was in the kitchen, and yet it was somehow impossible to make the words come to her lips.

Instead, rather angry to find herself being so submissive, she merely said:

"Very good, *Monsieur*, I shall of course, be waiting for your summons."

She went from the room as she spoke, and only when she was outside did she run as quickly as she could down the passage, up the stairs, and into the small Sitting-Room, where she found Gennie and Rover waiting for her.

******

Theresa cooked the *Marquis* an excellent luncheon and was amused to find that food she had not seen before was now pouring in from the estate.

From the Home Farm there came spring chickens, hams and newly-churned butter, and so much cream that she thought with a smile that they must be expecting the *Marquis* to bathe in it.

The game-keepers brought in hares and wild duck, and the foresters asked if the *Marquis* would like a young roe-deer killed.

There were fat pigeons, and trout from the stream, and the water-bailiffs offered to catch a salmon if she needed it from the nearest river that was only two miles away.

"If we cooked all this," Theresa said to Gennie, "it would feed a Regiment of soldiers!"

She took only what she wanted and gave the rest to the staff who were delighted with such attention.

Theresa had noticed however that when the *Marquis* was not there, they had lacked for very little.

The *Marquis*'s luncheon was over, and she was just finishing her own meal with Gennie when the message came that she had been expecting, again through the *Maître d'Hôtel.*

"Monsieur le Marquis wishes you, *M'mselle,* to join him in the stables. He intends to take the horses round the race-course."

Before Theresa could reply Gennie said to her in a whisper:

"Tell him you are indisposed. He has no right to ask such a thing of you."

"I want to ride, Theresa objected.

"But not with the *Marquis!* I'll not have it! We must leave!"

The *Maître d'Hôtel* was waiting and Theresa said:

"Will you inform *Monsieur le Marquis* that I will join him in the stables as soon as I have changed?"

As the door shut behind him Gennie jumped to her feet to say:

"Over my dead body, M'Lady! I'm not having you associating with that man! I'm going upstairs now to pack our boxes!"

"Do not be so stupid," Theresa replied. "The *Marquis* is not interested in me except that he thinks I am hiding something."

She paused to say:

"In fact, from what I said this morning, I should not be surprised if he thinks I am a spy!"

"A spy?" Gennie repeated.

"He thought it very strange that I should know so much about France and the intentions of the Prussians. You remember how often Mama spoke about it."

"Well, I don't like it! I dislike the whole thing!" Gennie said positively. "Whatever you say, M'Lady, he's still a Frenchman, and they are not to be trusted – any of them!"

"Nor is an Englishman!" Theresa added sharply. "They are all the same – English, French or Chinese – and you know that I hate them!"

Gennie was not listening.

They walked upstairs and Theresa was already beginning to change into her riding-habit when the old maid said:

"All I can say is – either the *Marquis* leaves here quickly, or else we do!"

"I am not listening to you!" Theresa replied.

She thought however, as she ran down the narrow staircase which led towards the stables, that it was a strange way for the *Marquis* de Sare to behave towards his Chef.

But whatever he did, she was not going to quarrel with him if she could possibly help it.

"I want to stay here! I want to stay!" she told herself.

She knew as she saw the *Marquis*'s horses being brought from the stables into the yard that it would be as agonising to leave them as it had been to leave her horses in England.

And now at the Château, there was an even greater attraction, and that was *Le Roi.*

******

The *Marquis*, as if he had been preparing an explanation for asking her to ride with him, said sharply in front of the grooms:

"I understand, *Mademoiselle,* that you have been exercising my horses for me in my absence. I therefore wish to be certain that you are capable of riding them in the way they should be ridden."

"I understand, *Monsieur*," Theresa replied in an equally cold voice, "and I can only hope that I will not commit too many errors of horsemanship."

She knew as she spoke that the old groom who had allowed her to ride in the first place was apprehensive in case he had done the wrong thing.

She smiled at him reassuringly as he helped her into the saddle of a magnificent chestnut horse that she had already found was one of the best jumpers in the stable.

Without even looking at the *Marquis* she started off in the direction of the race-course. He followed her and behind them came grooms leading the other horses they were to take over the jumps.

Once she started Theresa forgot everything but the joy of riding a magnificent animal which was superior to any horse she had ever ridden before in her whole life.

She took each fence in style and with nearly a foot to spare, and as she came round to the *Marquis*'s side she knew before he spoke that her performance had been flawless.

She did not ask for his approval, but merely dismounted and waited for the old groom to bring her the next horse she should ride.

Before she could mount however, the *Marquis* was taking his turn over the jumps and, although she told herself that she hated him, she had to admit that he was one of the best riders, if not the best, she had ever seen.

He seemed to be part of his horse and she realised he was riding one of the younger animals who was not so sure of himself as the others were.

She watched the *Marquis* seeing he had an expertise that was outstanding, and when he too had completed the course it was with difficulty that she prevented herself from congratulating him.

She knew it would be impertinent and instead, realising they were to take it in turns, she set off again determined to show him she could ride as well as he could.

It took a long time, but when every horse had been round once Theresa thought it would be impossible to find their equal anywhere either in France or in England.

Then as they rode back to the stables the *Marquis* said in a conversational manner for the first time since she had joined him:

"What I have to do now is to enlarge my stables, and I shall give orders that the work shall be put in hand immediately!"

"Why do you wish to do that?"

"Because after what you said about France and Prussia this morning, and because I entirely agree with your judgement I shall bring all my horses which have been trained at Chantilly, as well as the ones I keep in Paris, here."

She looked at him in a startled manner.

"Then you too believe that the danger is drawing nearer!"

"You told me the enemy is at the gate."

"That was a figure of speech!"

"Which unfortunately is true!"

Theresa drew in her breath.

"Then you really believe the horses will be safer here?"

"I am sure of it!" the *Marquis* replied. "The Château is so isolated that it was forgotten in the Revolution and remained untouched by Napoleon and by Wellington's invading English Army."

"That was fortunate!"

"Very fortunate, and of course, if we are talking of luck, it goes in threes. So I hope that Sare will be lucky for the third time running."

"I shall pray that will be true," Theresa said quietly.

"I intend to take no chances," the *Marquis* said. "I shall therefore fetch not only my horses but a great many other treasures as well away from Paris."

"Perhaps you are wise," Theresa said. "At the same time, *Monsieur*, perhaps we are being pessimistic."

The *Marquis* turned to look at her.

Their horses were moving side by side and he was very near to her.

Then he said:

"I have a strange feeling, and it is something I cannot substantiate, that while you have crystallised what I have been thinking myself, I needed a hand to point me in the right direction and tell me the right moment to go into action. That, *Mademoiselle*, is what you have done."

"I am glad I have been helpful," Theresa said.

She wanted to speak coldly and indifferently. But somehow her voice was soft and breathless, and there was undoubtedly a note of excitement in it.

Chapter Seven

"IT SAID in the newspaper today," Theresa said, "that laundry-women in Paris get two francs a day and a sewing-woman is lucky if she can earn three or five. I cannot imagine why people like you, *Monsieur*, do not do something about such appalling wages."

The *Marquis*, watching her accusing eyes, said nothing and Theresa went on:

"I am quite certain you are aware that sixteen hundred francs is considered quite cheap for a gown for the Empress and other *'Ladies'* in Paris!"

She emphasised the word *'Ladies'* and it was obvious from the scorn in her voice whom she meant.

"On the other hand," the *Marquis* objected, in his dry, calm voice, "when the Empress bought silk from Lyons it doubled the number of workers there, and the same applies to the lace-makers and those who make artificial flowers."

As Theresa considered this, the *Marquis* thought that

never in his whole life had he argued, or rather debated, with a woman in the same way that he did with her.

He might have done so with one of his male contemporaries who were aware of his personal interests, and to whom he talked privately in his own house or in some politician's office.

But he and Theresa had now talked, or rather duelled with each other in words, for five evenings, since he had come to the Château and as yet he had made no move to leave.

To Theresa it was the most fascinating and exciting experience she had ever known.

In fact, since the evenings of his arrival she was aware, if she was honest, that she had never been so happy.

Gennie of course had been horrified from the first moment that the *Marquis* had sent for her after dinner.

"You're to refuse to obey him, M'Lady!" she had declared. "Go straight to bed and say it's too late to see him now, and anything that has to be said can wait until morning."

Theresa had laughed.

"He would refuse to listen."

She was well aware what Gennie thought about it, and every night the old maid sat up until she came up to her bedroom, where she helped her undress and refused to leave until she heard her lock the door.

"The *Marquis* does not think of me as a woman but as his Chef!" she protested a dozen times.

"Chefs don't go into the Salon and have conversations with their Masters!" Gennie objected.

It was impossible to make her understand that the *Marquis* did not treat her like a woman, or as a Chef for that matter.

They talked of the political situation as it concerned France, and of course of his Menagerie.

Every morning they met in *Le Roi*'s enclosure, and however early Theresa tried to be, the *Marquis* was either there already, or else arrived within minutes of her.

He found excellent reasons for her to ride his horses, and

the old groom confessed that now he had so little exercising to do and with the weather getting warmer, his rheumatism had almost gone.

To Theresa it was a delight beyond words and she was having to admit to herself that the *Marquis* was very different from what she had expected.

Whatever he might do in Paris, as far as she was concerned he talked seriously and so interestingly that it was impossible not to hang on his words.

He never, in any way, made her feel that he regarded her as an attractive woman.

He praised the way she cooked, the way she rode, and was continually amazed at how she had captivated *Le Roi* so that the tiger divided his favours between them.

"I suppose I should be jealous," the *Marquis* said when *Le Roi* had bounded towards Theresa and rubbed himself against her in the same way as he did to his Master.

"I could not bear to leave him, but I suppose I ought to do so now that you are here."

She knew it would be a hard thing to do, and that she loved *Le Roi* more every day that she was with him.

"I think the best thing I can do," the *Marquis* remarked, "is to find *Le Roi* a wife, in which case he will doubtless ignore us both."

Theresa looked to see if he was joking. Then she asked:

"Would you really do that?"

"It is something I wish to talk to you about sometime," he replied, "but there is no hurry."

The way he spoke made it obvious he was not thinking of leaving the Château in the immediate future and Theresa felt her heart give a leap.

It was ridiculous for her not to admit frankly that riding with the *Marquis* was far more thrilling than riding alone.

Best of all, to talk to him was so absorbing that when she was cooking the dinner she found herself counting the minutes until the *Marquis* would withdraw to the Salon and send for her to join him.

Gennie might mutter that it was disgraceful and something

she should not do without a chaperon, but Theresa asked herself who was to know she was unchaperoned.

The *Marquis* never suggested in any way that he considered her a Lady.

'This is a different situation from anything that could arise if I were myself,' Theresa thought.

Today after the newspapers had arrived, she had realised the report on the wages in Paris would be a controversial subject that would stimulate both her and the *Marquis* into fighting with each other with words.

She knew they would talk as if they were Barristers with a Brief, from which each had to defend his own clients, and that when she started to speak of the poor, badly paid and down-trodden people of Paris the *Marquis* would champion the opposing view.

But she was aware from other conversations with him that actually he was extremely perturbed, as her mother had been, at the great gulf between the glittering extravagances of the rich, and the struggling hardship endured by the poor.

She was just thinking of what else she had read and how she could challenge the *Marquis* with it, when the door of the Salon opened and the *Maître d'Hôtel* came towards them.

"What is it?" the *Marquis* asked.

It was very unusual for any of the servants to come into the Salon after dinner, and once Theresa had joined him and a decanter of brandy had been left by his side, they were always left alone.

"Pardon, Monsieur," the *Maître d'Hôtel* said, "but a Gentleman has called to see *M'mselle!"*

"A gentleman?"

Theresa stiffened.

"I have shown him into the *Salon Bleu, M'mselle*, and he asks you to join him there immediately!"

Theresa went very pale and in a voice that trembled she asked:

"Did he . . give you his . . name?"

"Oui, M'mselle, he said he was *Milor'* Denholme!"

Theresa gave a little gasp and the *Marquis* said sharply:

"Wait outside!"

The *Maître d'Hôtel* went from the Salon closing the door behind him.

Theresa jumped to her feet.

"Hide me," she pleaded to the *Marquis* frantically. "Hide me! Please . . hide me!"

As she spoke she looked around the room as if she thought she might climb out of one of the windows into the garden.

"What does this man want with you?" the *Marquis* asked.

She could hardly attend to what he was saying because she was desperately thinking of where in the Château she could hide and how she and Gennie could get away without being seen.

Then as she realised that the *Marquis* was waiting for an answer to his question she said:

"He is my Uncle and . . my Guardian . . he is looking for me because . . I am rich . . and he wants my money!"

Her words seemed to fall over each other, and now she moved towards the window fearing if she left the room by the hall her Uncle might somehow see her.

Then the *Marquis* said quietly:

"Sit down! I will deal with this."

"You cannot!" Theresa said frantically. "There is nothing you can do except . . hide me. He has the . . law on his side, and I have to . . obey him."

"Leave it to me," the *Marquis* insisted.

As he spoke he rang a small gold bell that was on a table by his side.

Instantly the door opened and the *Maître d'Hôtel* stood waiting.

"Ask the Gentleman to come in here," the *Marquis* said.

"Very good, *Monsieur*."

Theresa gave a cry of protest.

"No . . no! You cannot . . do anything . . and he will . . take me away to England."

Once again she was sure that the only possible thing she could do would be to run from the Château and hide in the woods.

Then there was Rover to consider, and as if he knew how upset she was the small dog came from beneath her chair to stand looking up at her.

It was impossible to think clearly, she could only feel that everything that had made her happy had crashed about her.

It was as if the ceiling had fallen down on her head or the floor opened up beneath her feet to reveal a hideous chasm.

The next moment her Uncle came into the Salon.

As if he thought the name was too difficult to say, the *Maître d'Hôtel* did not announce him, and the Earl had eyes only for Theresa who, without realising what she was doing, had risen to her feet.

The *Marquis* on the other hand did not move.

He simply remained in his high-backed armchair apparently at his ease, as the Earl, wearing his travelling clothes, walked nearer and nearer to Theresa, an expression of anger on his somewhat florrid face.

"So here you are, Theresa," he said as he reached her, "and a nice dance you have led me! How dare you run away in that disgraceful fashion and cause me so much trouble in finding you!"

"H . . how did you . . find me . . Uncle Edward?"

She was trembling, but pride made her hold her chin high as if she refused to be bullied by him.

"You might say it was fate that revealed sooner than you must have expected, where you had gone," the Earl answered.

"But . . how could you have . . learned that?"

She was playing for time, hoping there might be some possible means by which she could defy her Uncle and refuse to go back to England with him.

"It may surprise you to learn that you are not as clever as you think you are," the Earl said with satisfaction. "I happened to ask a friend of mine, Lord Ludgrove, if he had a gun-dog I could take off his hands as mine are too old. Anyway, I need another one now that I have so much shooting."

He paused before he went on:

"Ludgrove informed me that unfortunately the only dog he could have let me have he had given to his mistress, a Frenchwoman who had been staying with him in England."

Theresa drew in her breath.

Now she began to understand what had happened.

"At my insistence, since I was very anxious to have the dog, Ludgrove wrote to this woman and asked her if she would sell it back to him. She replied that she had given it on her journey back to France to a *Mademoiselle* Theresa Beauvais, a pretty young girl whom she had sent to the *Marquis* de Sare because she wished to become a Chef."

"So that was how you . . found me!" Theresa exclaimed.

"That was how I found you!" the Earl repeated. "Now you will come back to England with me and marry your Cousin Rupert, as I have arranged, and I will make sure you do not run away again!"

There was a harsh note in his voice which told Theresa how incensed he was with her, and she felt almost as if he were putting hand-cuffs on her wrists, and there was nothing she could do but obey him.

Then as she began to say in a voice that trembled:

"B . . but . . I cannot . . I will not marry Rupert . . "

The *Marquis* interrupted her.

He spoke in English with a trace of an accent and his voice, strong and positive, seemed to vibrate through the room as he said:

"It is indeed, my Lord, quite impossible for Theresa to marry your son."

As if he was only just aware that the *Marquis* was present, the Earl turned to look at him. There was a frown between his eyes and his whole expression seemed to have darkened.

"This does not concern you, Sir!" he said. "And I can only imagine that as my niece is here in the Salon instead of being in the kitchen, which I understand is the position for which you employed her, she has learnt her standards of morality from her father, or perhaps she was corrupted by the prostitute who gave her Ludgrove's gun-dog!"

The way he spoke was so insulting that Theresa felt the

Marquis would not tolerate anything so offensive and would order them both to leave the Château immediately.

But when the Earl stopped speaking, the *Marquis* merely replied in a dry, impersonal tone that made him seem not only authoritative, but positively overwhelming.

"I cannot allow you, My Lord, even through ignorance to insult my wife."

For a moment there was complete silence.

Then Theresa's eyes widened until they seemed to fill her whole face and the Earl exclaimed incredulously:

"Your wife? Am I to understand that you have married my niece?"

The *Marquis* rose slowly to his feet.

"I regret, My Lord, that your long journey has been pointless," he said, "but I am sure there will be a train sometime before midnight which will convey you back to Paris."

"As I am Theresa's legal Guardian, she cannot marry without my consent," the Earl said heavily, as if it was the first thought that came into his head after the shock of what he had just learned.

"I cannot believe, My Lord," the *Marquis* replied, "that you are prepared to fight me in the French Courts, which I am certain will prove unsympathetic and you will find it a tedious, long-drawn-out and extremely expensive action."

The Earl was defeated, and he knew it.

Then as he obviously fumbled for words, trying frantically to think out how he could assert himself, the *Marquis* said:

"Allow me to escort you to your carriage."

He walked ahead of him down the Salon and the Earl looked at Theresa as if he wished to curse her only to find no words with which to do so.

Instead he followed the *Marquis*, walking heavily as if he was suddenly tired and dispirited.

Theresa could hear their footsteps across the hall but so soon did the *Marquis* come back into the Salon and shut the door, that she was sure he had left the servants to hand the Earl into his carriage.

She had not moved but was standing, her whole body trembling, her fingers locked together.

The *Marquis* hardly looked at her but seated himself in the chair he had just vacated and said in French:

"I wish you had trusted me with your secret! It made it more difficult, but I think your Uncle is aware there is nothing he can do."

He was speaking so calmly that Theresa suddenly became aware that she had been holding her breath.

As if her legs would no longer support her, she sat down on a chair.

"You were . . wonderful!" she stammered in a voice that quivered. "But now you must . . tell me where I can go . . because when he finds out that what you told him is not true, he will certainly . . come back."

The *Marquis* did not answer and she went on:

"He needs my fortune desperately in order to keep up the family house and estate."

"Your father was the late Earl," the *Marquis* stated. "I met him once when I was in Paris."

Theresa's attitude changed and her voice was hard as she replied:

"Papa . . enjoyed the . . gaieties of Paris . . and he only returned home when he wanted . . more money from my mother . . to spend on the . . women he entertained there!"

"So that is why you hate Paris!"

"How can I do anything else?" Theresa asked. "Papa . . broke Mama's heart. She loved him and she did not realise when they . . married that he was only . . interested in her money!"

She drew in her breath before she said furiously:

"How could I suffer as Mama suffered by marrying my Cousin Rupert, whom actually I have not even met, simply because I am rich? It makes me . . sick to . . think of it!"

"Of course it does!" the *Marquis* agreed.

"You understand . . you really understand?"

"Of course I do! But your Uncle is obviously very determined to force you to do as he wishes."

"He has the law of England on his side," Theresa said bitterly, "and because he wishes to live in the grand manner, if he once learns that I am free, he will find me somehow."

The fear was back in her eyes as she was thinking that perhaps she and Gennie should leave early the next morning.

"The world is a . . big place," she said as if she spoke to herself. "If I keep moving . . if I perhaps . . go to Africa . . he will never find me there."

"You cannot spend the rest of your life in hiding!"

"I have to . . at least until Rupert marries somebody else! If I run short of money I can, as you know, earn my living as a cook."

"I have a much better, much safer way of making sure your Uncle does not continue to persecute you."

"What is that?"

She was not very hopeful that the *Marquis* would have a solution, and she was sure that her Uncle would take legal advice as to whether there was anything he could do to get her supposed marriage annulled.

He would quickly discover that the *Marquis* had lied.

Nevertheless, because she could not have talked with the *Marquis* all these evenings without realising how clever he was and how sharp his brain, there was just a faint hope in her large eyes as she looked at him.

She was wondering if conceivably he might have a solution, even though it appeared to her to be impossible.

To her surprise he rose from his chair and holding out his hand, drew her to her feet.

He led her across the room to the window and pulling back the curtains opened one of the long French windows that led onto the terrace outside.

Without speaking they walked out together.

The moon was rising up the sky and it cast a silver light over the formal garden that lay before them, leading up to the large stone fountain which was no longer playing.

There was the fragrance of night stock and the only sound was that of the crickets.

It was so beautiful, so unearthly, that Theresa drew in her

breath, thinking she must imprint this loveliness on her mind.

They stood together for a moment in silence. Then the *Marquis* said:

"I think this means something to you, as it does to me."

"It is . . so beautiful!" Theresa replied. "Wherever I go, I shall feel it living in my heart for all time, and I shall never forget."

"And will you think too of *Le Roi?"*

"How could I ever forget him? And perhaps . . when I am gone . . he will miss me a little."

"I know he will," the *Marquis* agreed, "and I shall miss you too, so I suggest you stay here."

Theresa made a sound that was half a sob.

"That is . . what I long to do, but you know it is impossible! Uncle Edward will fight violently to get my fortune . . he will never give it up. Perhaps when he gets to Paris he will learn the . . truth that we are not . . married and come back."

She was trembling again as she thought how easily this might happen.

The *Marquis* looked at her in the moonlight, then moved a little nearer before he said:

"That is why it would be very foolish not to agree to my suggestion of how you can be safe and escape from your Uncle now and for ever."

"How can I . . do that?"

"You can marry me! I have a great dislike of telling lies!"

It was something that had never entered Theresa's mind.

She stared at the *Marquis* as if she had misunderstood what he said before she asked:

"What . . are you saying? I . . I do not understand?"

"You said you would miss the garden, the Château and *Le Roi*," the *Marquis* said quietly. "Perhaps it is a presumption but I have a feeling, Theresa, you would also miss me!"

"Of course I . . would! It has been so . . exciting talking to you, and afterwards when I am . . alone I remember . . everything we have . . said to each other."

"There is so much more I want to talk about with you, and

I am sure you have provocative arguments on innumerable subjects on which we can argue with each other."

"And because of . . that you have . . asked me to . . marry you?"

"There are other reasons," the *Marquis* replied, "but there is an urgency for your marriage which neither of us can ignore."

"But . . I have sworn I would . . never marry! I swore it on my mother's grave, and . . I hate men!"

"But you love *Le Roi*, my horses and of course Rover! They are all of the male sex."

"That is . . different."

"I hoped I was different too, and that you no longer hate me as you did when I first came home."

"You . . know I . . hated you?" Theresa asked in surprise.

"I saw it in your eyes, and now that I know why you loathe and despise Paris I understand your feelings. But I had hoped you were beginning to think that I was not tarred with the same brush."

"No . . no . . of course not . . and as I have said . . you are different."

"If in fact you do not hate me. Then what do you feel about me?"

He was speaking in the same quiet, rather dry tone in which they had conducted all their arguments, and almost as if he forced her to do so, Theresa searched for an answer.

It was then, like a blinding light that was part of the moonlight and yet more intense, she knew that what she felt for the *Marquis* was very much the same as what she felt for *Le Roi.*

It was love!

Because love for a man was something she had never experienced before, she had not recognised it.

She knew now she had been very stupid in not being aware that she had awoken with an irrepressible excitement each morning knowing she would see the *Marquis* when she went to find *Le Roi.*

It was a joy beyond words to ride with him in the afternoons and, best of all, to be with him after dinner.

It was love which made the hours move slowly when she did not see him, and love which gave her a feeling of excited expectancy as dinner came to an end and she knew it was only a question of minutes before she would be with him in the Salon.

Of course she loved him!

She had not realised that what she was feeling was love, although the happiness which invaded her whole body like sunshine sprang from him.

Now for the first time, she was aware he was a man and a very attractive one, and she could feel his vibrations coming towards her, and they made her feel shy.

She walked forward to put her hand as if for support against the stone balustrade and looked down into the garden.

She was aware that her whole body was pulsating with a strange sensation she had never known before. It made her want to run away.

At the same time she wanted to stay.

"I have something to tell you, Theresa," the *Marquis* said beside her.

"I am . . listening."

"I expect you have been told that I was married for a very short time, and it was a disaster. Because I suffered acutely from the experience in my pride more than anything else, I swore I would never marry again, unless I fell in love."

Theresa was listening, but she did not look at him, and he went on:

"As the years passed and I found the love I wanted was very different from the amusement I enjoyed with the women with whom I associated, I began to believe I would never find what I sought, and was determined therefore to remain free."

He paused for a moment. Then he continued:

"And yet I wanted the love that seemed out of reach. Without ever putting it into words I was most conscious that it was missing from my life when I was at home."

He looked away from Theresa out into the garden spread out before them and continued:

"This has always been my real home, where I decided I would bring my bride, if I really loved her. Because she would fill a secret shrine in my heart which has always been linked with Sare, we would live here quietly with my animals and our children. And everything that Paris stood for would be very easily forgotten."

"Could you . . really do . . that?" Theresa asked.

"It is what I intend to do, now that I have the right person to do it with me."

There was a silence which made Theresa hold her breath. Then he said:

"When I saw you with your arms around *Le Roi* I knew that unexpectedly, incredibly, the woman I had been seeking for so long was already in my home, and waiting for me!"

"That . . cannot be . . true . . I cannot believe . . it!"

"It is true."

"And you . . really knew . . at that moment . . that you . . loved me?"

She found it hard to say the words and the *Marquis* replied:

"I did not realise at first that what I felt was love, but behind *Le Roi* and you I saw like a picture, the snowy peaks of the Himalayas and that was a sign for me that something very strange and very special was happening which could not be ignored."

The way he spoke was very moving, and almost as if she must fight against the strange ecstasy that was sweeping through her, Theresa said:

"I . . I am sure I am not the . . right person for you to . . marry."

"Who can decide that except myself?" the *Marquis* asked. "You can have no idea, Theresa, how difficult it has been these last few days not to tell you how beautiful you are, and how much I want you."

She looked at him in surprise.

"You have never said . . anything to make me think you . . even noticed what I . . looked like."

"I had seen the hatred in your eyes," the *Marquis* replied, ''and I heard the condemnation in your voice when you took me to task not only for my sins, but also for all the sins of Paris. You really made me a scapegoat!''

Theresa gave a little laugh that trembled.

''How . . could I have known . . at first . . that you were so different?''

The *Marquis* turned towards her.

''You have still not told me what you think of me now.''

As he spoke his arms went round her and he pulled her close to him.

He felt the quiver that went through her, then with his mouth close to hers, he said:

''Answer me!''

''I . . I think you are . . wonderful . . magnificent!'' Theresa whispered.

The last word was lost against his lips, and as he kissed her Theresa knew that not only was she in love, but it was more marvellous, more perfect, more glorious than anything she could have possibly imagined.

As the *Marquis* drew her closer and still closer, and his kiss became more demanding, more possessive, she felt as if she had become a part of him, and he swept away everything that had made her afraid.

She was safe, she was his, and they were enveloped in a dazzling light that could only be part of the Divine.

******

It was a long time later that the *Marquis* drew Theresa back through the open window into the Salon.

''I must send you to bed, my darling,'' he said, ''because now I have a lot of plans to make.''

''Plans?''

He looked down at her with the candlelight on her face and thought it was impossible for any woman to look so beautiful, so radiant, with a spirituality which he recognised came from her heart and soul.

It was something he had never found before in any of the

women with whom he had sought pleasure in Paris.

Now he knew he had been looking in the wrong place for what he sought.

At the same time it seemed incredible that he should find anybody so beautiful, so pure and innocent, which was exactly what he had always wanted, here in the Château that had always meant more to him than all his other possessions put together.

He knew that just as Theresa would be starting a new life as a married woman and his wife, so he would be starting a new chapter in his own life.

It would be entirely different from anything he had ever done before.

He drew her to the sofa and they sat down as he said:

"I want you to go to bed and dream of me, but not to hurry to get up in the morning because I have to arrange for my Chaplain to marry us in the Chapel, and I think that should be about noon."

"Y . . you are . . quite sure it is . . right for you to marry me?"

"I am quite sure because it is what we both want, and we will find a happiness that has nothing to do with money, with amusement or anything except that we are man and wife, and belong to each other."

"That is what I always . . wanted . . and did not . . know it."

The *Marquis* smiled.

"I have so much to teach you, my precious, and it will be the most exciting thing I have ever done in my whole life!"

"Do you . . mean that? Do you . . really mean it?"

"I told you that if possible, I always speak the truth, and I swear to you that I love you in a way I have never loved anybody else. I have been searching for you for so long that I can hardly believe I have at last been fortunate enough to find you."

He kissed her again as if to make sure she understood and she knew that the ecstasy his lips gave her was more eloquent than anything he could say in words.

"I love you! I . . love you!" she whispered. "I never thought I would ever say such a thing to . . a man!"

"I want you to say it a thousand times," he replied, "until you are quite sure it is true, and think of nothing else except that we shall be very happy! We have a great deal to do to make this a perfect background for our love."

Theresa looked at him enquiringly and he said:

'First, as you know, I am determined to bring my horses and my other treasures here from Paris, and I have the feeling it has to be done very quickly in case we leave it too late."

Theresa pressed herself against him as if she was afraid, and the *Marquis* went on:

"Then we will create the finest Menagerie of wild animals in the whole of France. We may have to travel a lot in order to find many of them, but I think that is something we will both enjoy."

"It will be the most . . wonderful thing to do," Theresa said, "because I will . . be with you."

The *Marquis* kissed her forehead before he went on:

"After that, I have a feeling, my lovely one, that we shall be needed, both of us, to help reconstruct, if what we both fear happens, what will need to be a new France."

"You mean . . after the . . war with Prussia?" Theresa asked with a tremor in her voice.

"That, and if the People's Revolution we also fear comes to pass everything will be changed," the *Marquis* said quietly. "There will be a new *Régime* in France, when every Frenchman will have to try to build anew the country he loves."

Because he was saying exactly what Theresa thought a man should feel about his native land, she looked up at him adoringly.

"Let me help you," she pleaded, "please . . let me help you."

"Whatever I aspire to do," the *Marquis* replied, "I need your help, your guidance, your inspiration, and my precious one, your love – the love that makes us both aware that we are incomplete without each other."

Theresa gave a little cry of sheer happiness.

"That is what I want you to say and want you to think, and although you are so wise and so clever, perhaps I can assist you a little, if only by looking after you . . and loving you."

The *Marquis* kissed her and it was impossible to say any more.

Only when there was a fire in his eyes and he was aware that he had awakened a little flame within Theresa, did he pull her to her feet.

"Go to bed, my precious," he said, and his voice was curiously unsteady. "I want to stay here kissing you all night, but you must look beautiful tomorrow as my bride – even more beautiful than you look already, although I am sure that would be impossible!"

Because he made Theresa feel as if she was floating among the stars and it was hard to come back to earth, she let him lead her across the Salon.

Only when they reached the door did he kiss her again, demandingly, fiercely and possessively, until he released her to take her to the bottom of the stairs.

Then he kissed her hand, and as the night-footman was on duty they did not speak, only looked for a moment into each other's eyes before Theresa went up the stairs while he stood watching her.

Then as she reached the first landing she heard him sending for the *Maître d'Hôtel* and giving sharp, authoritative orders which she knew concerned their wedding.

******

Theresa slept dreamlessly and awoke to find that the sun was coming through the sides of the curtains and Rover was licking her hand as if to tell her it was time to get up.

She jumped out of bed and went to the window to draw back the curtains, and as she did so she sent a prayer that was like a paean of praise up to the sky.

She was in love!

Today she would be married, and it was everything she had longed for, secretly within her heart, even while she had vowed that it would never happen.

"I am to be married," she wanted to cry to the world, the sky, the birds, the flowers and of course to *Le Roi.*

As she thought of the tiger, she imagined that the *Marquis* was like him. Frightening, dangerous, and unpredictable except to someone he loved. Then he could be tender, gentle, protective and very, very loving.

"I am . . in love with a Tiger!" she whispered and laughed at her fantasy.

It was Gennie who brought her breakfast to her room saying as she did so:

"I don't know what's happening, M'Lady, but *Monsieur* gave orders that you were to sleep 'til you awoke! I heard you pulling back the curtains just now, and it's ten o'clock!"

"Is it really as late as that?" Theresa asked. "Then there are only two hours, Gennie, before I am to be married!"

"Married?"

At first Gennie could not believe it, then as she learnt it was the truth, tears ran down her cheeks.

"It's everything I've wanted for you, M'Lady, everything! I've learnt since I've been here what a fine man *Monsieur* is – very different from what we thought of him, and what was said when we were in Paris."

Theresa suspected that Gennie had been listening to the *Marquis*'s valet who she had learned had been with him for a long time and adored the ground he walked on.

It was the valet who brought her half-an-hour later the exquisite lace veil which had been in the Sare family for generations.

With it was a velvet box which contained a diamond tiara.

It was fashioned like a wreath of flowers and so beautiful that Theresa knew it was exactly what she wanted as a bride.

Fortunately in one of her trunks there was a white evening-gown, which she had thought far too elaborate to wear at the Château, but which her mother had bought for her before she became ill.

She was sure now that her mother must have had a premonition about it, because she had said:

"It is much more elaborate and very much more expensive than we usually buy, my dearest, but when I saw it I felt you would need it for a very special occasion, so we shall just have to wait and see."

When Theresa finally walked into the beautiful little Chapel, which had been built at the same time as the Château and which the gardeners had decorated with what seemed to be every white flower in the garden, she was sure her mother was near her.

She would be glad that not only had her daughter found a man she loved, but also that he was French.

Perhaps one day, Theresa thought, they could seek out her mother's relatives, but all she wanted at the moment was to be alone with her husband and in his home which was for both of them a Château of Love.

After the marriage service was over and they had eaten a light luncheon, and were alone, they walked out into the garden.

Looking at her the *Marquis* said:

"Could any man have a more beautiful wife? Could any man love you more than I do, my darling?"

"It is all so wonderful!" Theresa breathed. "And yet . . I felt that there was someone missing at our wedding."

"Who was that?"

"Le Roi! He brought us together, and I was thinking this morning that if you had not seen me with *Le Roi* the first day you returned, you might have never realised that your Chef was a woman and very determined to keep out of your sight."

"I think even if I had not seen you I would have been conscious that you were in the Château," the *Marquis* replied. "If we are not together I feel your vibrations as I think you feel mine, and my sweet, adorable wife, the only real mistake I have made in marrying you is that we now have to find a new Chef!"

Theresa laughed.

"Poor *Monsieur* Brantome! He will have to start all over again! But while he is doing that Gennie, who really is very good, has already offered to cook for us, except when I want to make you something very, very special."

The *Marquis* laughed.

"I will not allow you to leave me to go into the kitchen or anywhere else! I want you with me every day, every night, every hour and every second. Heart of my Heart, how is it possible that I have lived so long without you?"

He put his arms around her and kissed her, until she felt as if the garden was whirling around them, they were high in the sky and inside the sun.

"I love you! I love you!"

The words seemed to be echoed in the song of the birds, the fragrance of the flowers, and the vibrations they felt as they stood under the blossom-covered trees.

Then as the *Marquis* raised his head and she knew his heart was beating as excitedly as hers, she said:

"There is one thing I must do, my wonderful husband."

"What is that?" the *Marquis* asked.

"I must show *Le Roi* my wedding-gown, and he must see you also in all your finery!"

The *Marquis* laughed.

"Of course! And perhaps it will encourage him to want a bride of his own which I am now determined to find for him!"

"You must do that, and when they have cubs we will bring them up to love us."

"We will have a family of animals, and a family of our own," the *Marquis* said.

He loved the blush that came to his wife's face and the shy look in her eyes as she whispered:

"I hope we can have a . . large one so that our children need never be . . lonely as I was with . . only the animals and the birds to talk to."

"I will be very generous," the *Marquis* answered, "and let you have as many sons and daughters as you wish."

He gave a laugh that was a very tender, loving sound.

But there was a fire in his eyes and as Theresa looked up everything else was forgotten. Everything but the knowledge that she was now safe.

He kissed her again and was at first very gentle. Then the softness of her lips made him more passionate and there was a fire in them which seemed to Theresa to set her whole body alight.

It answered a strange ecstasy which made her want to be closer and still closer to the *Marquis* until she was no longer herself but entirely his.

She did not understand how it could happen, but it was what she yearned for and the flames inside her made it an irrepressible need.

Then abruptly the *Marquis* drew her back into the Salon.

"*Le Roi* will have to wait," he said. "I want you my beautiful bride, and as I have waited a million years for you, I cannot wait any longer."

Theresa made a little murmur of excitement but she did not speak and he lifted her up in his arms.

"You are mine!" he said triumphantly. "I own your heart, your soul, your mind and your exquisite body now, and until the end of time."

He carried her across the hall and up the stairs that led to her bedroom.

It was the State bedroom which had been occupied by every *Marquis* de Sare since the Château was built.

It was a beautiful room, and now, filled with flowers, it was a fairytale bower for a bride.

As the *Marquis* set Theresa down he lifted off first her tiara and then her veil before he went to lock the door.

Theresa stood by the big four-poster bed with its canopy of golden cupids with her hands pressed against her breasts.

The *Marquis* turned round. Then as he moved towards her he asked:

"What is wrong? What is worrying you?"

For a moment she could not answer until she moved swiftly towards him like a lost child and hid her face against his shoulder.

"What is it, my precious?"

So softly that he could hardly hear she replied:

"I am . . frightened."

"Of me?"

"No, not . . really but . . . "

"What frightens you? Tell me."

It was obviously difficult for her to reply, but at last she said, still in a very low voice:

"I am not sure . . what a man and a woman . . do when . . they make love . . but suppose when we do . . you are . . disappointed and leave . . me?"

She was thinking of her father and the fear in her voice was very revealing.

The *Marquis* picked her up again in his arms and laid her on top of the bed.

Then he took off his tight-fitting evening-coat which every Frenchman wears at his wedding, and lying down beside her put his arm round her shoulders.

Her cheek was against his fine linen shirt and Theresa could feel the warmth and strength of his body and felt a little thrill run through her.

"Let us talk about this, my darling," the *Marquis* said, "which I would have done before we were married if it had not been so imperative for you to become my wife as quickly as possible."

He pulled her a little closer before he went on in his deep voice:

"I love you, and as I have said before it is very different to what I have felt for any woman in the past."

He paused as if he was feeling for words before he continued:

"Although I want you passionately as a woman, I also revere, respect and worship you spiritually."

Theresa made a little movement against him but she did not speak and he went on:

"I will teach you about the passions of love, my adorable little wife, which will be very thrilling for me, and I will be very gentle, so as not to hurt or frighten you."

He kissed her forehead as he spoke.

"But," he said after a moment, "*together* we will seek the spiritual side of our marriage which comes from the Divine, for which we both need the help and guidance of God."

"Do . . you really . . mean that?"

"I do, and it is something neither I nor any other man would look for or find with the women you hate and despise in Paris."

Now Theresa looked up at the *Marquis*, her eyes seeking his.

"You are . . sure, quite sure . . I will . . not bore you . . so that you . . will go . . back to them?"

"If I go to Paris you will come with me. I am no longer interested in the gaieties which are deliberately baited traps for rich men who are unhappy or alone."

The *Marquis* stopped speaking and as Theresa thought over what he said, he added quietly:

"We have rushed into marriage because of your Uncle, but, my precious, we have our whole lives in front of us. If it will make you feel more secure, we will go on being simply friends, and only when you ask to do so, will I make you mine!"

Theresa stared at him in astonishment, and then she knew that no man could be so kind, so understanding and so unselfish.

Pure and inexperienced she was woman enough to realise she excited the *Marquis* and she had known as he carried her upstairs how greatly he wanted her.

But he was ready to control his desires and think only of the spiritual side of their marriage until she was ready.

'He is wonderful!'

Her love for him rose like a tidal wave and impulsively, without thinking, she said what was in her heart:

"I love you . . I love you with . . all of me . . and I do not want to wait . . so please . . please make me . . yours!"

The *Marquis* turned round and as Theresa's head fell back on the pillow, he looked down at her.

"Are you certain that is what you want?"

His voice was very deep.

"Quite . . certain," Theresa answered, "but since I am so . . ignorant . . you will not . . let me do anything . . wrong?"

"I adore your ignorance, your innocence and your purity," the *Marquis* said hoarsely.

Then he kissed her at first gently and tenderly until, as he felt her lips respond and her arms went round his neck, his kisses became more demanding.

For Theresa it was as if the Heavens opened and a dazzling light enveloped them both.

It seemed to strike through her body, giving her an ecstasy which was so intense it was half an indescribable rapture and half pain.

Then as the *Marquis* kissed her neck, and the hollow between her breasts, she heard herself cry:

"Love me . . Oh, my wonderful, magnificent . . husband. I love you . . I love you . . please . . please love me!"

Then there was only the fragrance of the flowers, the singing of the angels, and the Glory of the Divine – which is the real Love of God.